TALLAHASSEE'S MANUAL ON ARCANE ARTIFACTS

BOOK TWO OF THE DRC FILES

KEVIN A DAVIS

Inkd
Publishing

For April
My wife has to put up with way more than anyone should, but she tolerates my constant ramblings about my writing, the sudden need for developmental help, and the endless proofing. Thank you.

In Memory of David Farland.
A guiding teacher who was always passionate about mentorship and writing. You are loved and missed.

TALLAHASSEE'S MANUAL ON ARCANE ARTIFACTS

CONTENTS

INTRODUCTION

This is the continuing story of Kristen Winters, first a mother, also a witch, and formerly a lead detective for the police force in Grand Junction.

Now, she's part of the Department of Realm Containment where they deal with the worst to come out of the six realms intersecting with Earth.

This second episode gives us a deeper glimpse into the workings of Kristen's world, and the dangers it contains. The case begins in Tallahassee, and the DRC team engages in another paranormal procedural to determine what or who is shattering peoples' bones.

CHAPTER

ONE

Wendall Landon strode down the Tallahassee sidewalk along Park Avenue. He sipped his hot coffee with a wince, then juggled it to his other hand. They never made the cup sleeves thick enough to bear the heat. He couldn't taste it over his burnt tongue, but the rich, sweet-tinged aroma seemed right.

He had a client due at ten past noon in the office. Wendall often ate an early lunch to accommodate a customer's midday availability, especially since he'd hooked the man for an overly broad policy.

The light at Monroe Street changed, and Wendall sped his pace to make it across the crosswalk. The cars along Park Avenue started forward, and traffic was light enough that a jerk wouldn't try for a turn and cut him off. To his left, a black BMW sped straight down Park Avenue. A quick glance over his shoulder proved he'd have no more traffic to contend with. Satisfied that he'd make the crosswalk and his appointment on time, Wendall tried for a second sip, focusing on the steam.

As he stepped past the bricked corner of the building, he had only a momentary warning as the tip of black boot appeared from the other side. A tall man wearing a cowboy hat bustled down Monroe Street with no regard for Wendall's rightful passage or his momentum toward the crosswalk's white crossing light.

Wendall managed to move his lips away from the cup, but the man barged into him, turning only slightly to brush his back against Wendall. The cup slapped onto Wendall's chest, the cheap lid popped free, and steaming coffee poured onto his pale blue shirt.

Pain flaring across his chest, Wendall stumbled two steps forward, shoving the cup away and burning his left hand as it sloshed out. "What the hell is wrong with you?"

He shifted the cup to his right hand, pulled the shirt away from his burned skin, and shook what he could off his cuffs.

The man, dressed in a dark blue T-shirt and jeans, crossed Park Avenue against the light, never looking back. He strolled toward the park in the middle as if he hadn't just stained Wendall's shirt and possibly caused third or some such degree burns.

"Asshole." Wendall glanced around, but the only witness was a mousy woman in a pink blouse gawking in front of the mailbox. If he didn't have an appointment that he had to clean up for, he would have chased the man down and called the police. He let loose a stream of profanity toward the man's back, yelling louder as they became less imaginative.

Tossing his half-empty cup into the planters in front of the woman and mailbox, he stepped into the crosswalk. A horn blasted to his left as a gray Volvo screeched to a stop at the intersection, angled with the intention of turning onto Monroe Street.

Wendall shouted at the driver and threw him the finger. Then, as he continued along the crosswalk, he screamed a different note.

A distinct snap sounded through his bones and ears. Pain raced up his ankle. Like a forest fire compared to a match, it eclipsed the burns on his chest and hands. He started to fall.

Flashes of light dotted his vision as another bone broke in his lower leg. He felt his flesh tear as it ripped through. The bricks of the crosswalk loomed closer, and his eyes caught the blue cuff of his right hand as it reached out to break his fall.

Though his scream died, the horn continued. Wendall's legs and hips shifted, shearing muscles and nerves. His chest grew stiff as his back buckled.

Instead of catching his fall, his hand crumpled in front of his face. First his thumb and knuckles blended together in an unnatural mass, then bones snapped in his wrist. A shard ripped through the skin of his forearm. His blue sleeve pressed against a darkening splotch.

The pain ceased when his chin broke on the brickwork. He could see the gray mortar between worn red brick. The faded paint of the stripe stretched beyond his vision. The horn finally stopped.

The woman babbled inanely. A car door opened.

A man spoke in a hushed voice. "I've got to go. Some asshole just fell."

Help me, thought Wendall. He couldn't breathe.

Footsteps scurried to him. Finally, someone was going to help.

A distinctly foreign voice spoke from above. "Mister, are you okay?" The voice seemed distant, as if they were yelling down a corridor, but Wendall only heard a whisper.

A shadow passed overhead, and the red brick darkened, and darkened.

"Lord, help him." The man with the accent spoke so quietly. "Don't move," he said.

I can't, thought Wendall. The shadow swallowed the bricks, the sounds, and Wendall.

TWO

I waited as pages spit out of the printer in the office of the Department of Realm Containment, a Consociation team hidden inside Atlanta's FBI building, where the nasty electric and toner fumes hung like a cloud. The day had been near its end when the case hit. Another report from the Tallahassee police describing three witnesses who agreed that the man had not been hit by the only questionable car at the scene. In my skimming, I'd yet to get the gist of what *had* happened.

David hadn't joined Finn in Marie's office. Instead, he sauntered across the floor behind me, barely rippling the seams of his immaculately tailored suit. His short brown bob of a ponytail bounced just out of reach of his neck. "I had a wonderful evening planned with a dashing young woman named Alexandria."

"So you mentioned."

"Alexandria's going to be heartbroken, as she should be." David waited for me to respond as the copies of the last page were printing. His unnaturally handsome face held his usual smirk, accented with reddish lips against his pale skin.

He continued, becoming more outlandish because I'd already told him to shut up about her today. "Legs up to here, hair down to there." His long stride took him past all three of our desks, as if he might finally go into Marie's office. Instead, he spun and studied my reaction.

I turned with the last collated printout and headed for Marie's door. My shorter and wider stature took up more of the space between the cabinets and desks than his did; his stance put him squarely in my way.

As I approached, he leaned forward, smiling until his vampire cuspids showed. "Brow like a queen, skin you would die for, blue eyes like a sunlit bay." David tugged at his dark jacket with pale fingers and feigned a mock insult as I squeezed past without comment. "What's that look for?"

I glanced back, restraining a smile. "That's how eye roll."

As I opened Marie's office door, David snorted. "That was horrible."

The room appeared both cluttered with books and items, yet large. Well-proportioned like me, Marie sat behind a worn wooden desk studying her monitor. Her white shirt stood sharp against her tan skin and dark suit. She didn't glance as I entered, but she shifted her chair back slightly.

Wearing a dark suit but no tie, Finn sat in the back left of the office at the table where the shelves lining the walls formed a corner. His dreads jostled as he noted me, and a warm smile softened his brown face. He'd been moody for the past couple of weeks since we'd stopped the cryptids from popping out of Tarus. I believed he was having trouble with his husband Gary, but we never discussed it, even after work.

Marie raised her bald, brown head, edged her chair back a little further, snapped her eyes off her screen, and put out a hand for a copy of the reports. "Folders already." Her tone said she approved, as I had known she would.

David snorted. "Where's mine?"

I slipped into a chair across from Finn and kept the purple folder while dropping the other two on the table. I liked the hue. Finn took the yellow one, and I smiled.

David grumbled as he tucked back an expensive tie before taking his seat and picking up his brown folder. The room had a woody, pleasant scent, but I caught David's faint odor of death.

Searching for the orange cat, Tiberius, I peered beside Marie's red sofa, among the shelves, and under the desk. I didn't find it before she spun to face us with her report open.

"Wheels up in forty-three. Wendall Landon, white male, aged thirty-eight, insurance salesman. Died on scene in Tallahassee at 12:28 p.m. today at the intersection of Monroe Street and Park Ave, over two hours and fifty minutes ago."

I twirled curls in my hair, skimming ahead on the reports. There wasn't much there.

Marie flipped a page. "Paramedics and police assumed a vehicular incident due to the location in a crosswalk and broken bones. Death believed from a spinal injury. Police ruled out the vehicle, a gray Volvo XC60 T5 . . ." She trailed off as the details drifted into the positioning of the vehicle, which had *not* hit the man.

"Three-quarters down," I said.

She continued reading. "Coroner found the bones unusually brittle during their attempt to store the body for autopsy. Our people intercepted an email in which the coroner detailed the injuries and condition as unnatural. The case has been transferred to us. Police photos are being retained by a local detective, James Dee, who has resisted release to local FBI."

David giggled, but silenced quickly.

Marie peered up under her eyebrows without lifting her head. "Something funny?"

"C'mon, Pyre. Jimmy D."

She ignored him and returned her gaze to her papers, paged through the witnesses' statements, then checked the time. "What do we have?"

Finn cocked his head when I looked at him. I cleared my throat and spoke. "Well, a crushing spell from the Dur-Alf realm would also mash softer organs. Will Herta have the body to autopsy?"

Marie dug in her jacket pocket, pulled out her comms, and tucked it into her ear. I had mine in my purse, fully charged. She spoke with her usual calm firmness. "Tomas. What's the status of the body?"

She frowned at his response. "Let me know when Stacey clears that up. We need the body."

Marie and her direct boss, Stacey, always had some office conflict below the surface of their relationship. I found it difficult, if not unsurprising, that the team was successful despite Stacey's obvious resistance. I'd seen this in other departments and wondered how some people never got fired.

Frowning thoughtfully, Marie spoke with measured patience. "Dig into the local department and coroner's office. I want to know what's actually going on." She didn't seem willing to wait for her superior's resolution and might search for other avenues.

Marie noted my curious gaze. "Stacey's working with

the local FBI on some issue with the paperwork." She nudged her chin toward Finn. "What do you have?"

"Mahakala's quartz, Pyre." Finn smiled apologetically to me. "A Tibetan artifact formed during some darker times. Crushes the bones of your enemies according to the only description we have. Hypothesized to have been built with Earth realm incantations. There are three incidents preindustrial age when it . . ."

"Wheels up in thirty-nine. Explain during the flight. David?"

"Obviously, Pyre, a nasty little dwarf or even a . . ." He gestured to Marie's ear then his own.

"Someone who can use Earth realm magic." Marie clarified with a glare. "That would twist the Consociation. There hasn't been an incident in eighty-three years."

Once again, I felt sorely lacking in my knowledge. In two weeks with nothing to do, I'd skimmed through enough of Tomas's database to know I'd never finish. "So, Earth realm magic can break bones, but leave the rest of the body intact?"

Marie thoughtfully nodded, distracted. "Even target just nerves, brain, lung, etc. Any creature."

David tapped on the table, his usually handsome face skewed into a frown. "Don't forget blood."

As Marie stood, we all scrambled from our chairs. "First we clean up this mess with the body and local LEOs. We'll need deeper interviews than these." She waved the folder of reports. "Then we reassess."

I led the way past her desk. The coroner's description had been horrifying; Wendall's bones had continued to break even long after his death. Rigor mortis might help, until it released. Between the two useful suggestions offered to Marie, I hoped it turned out to be some talisman rather than evil dwarves or merfolk.

"I can drive, Pyre," Finn offered behind me.

Marie huffed. "Nope."

I raised my eyebrows as I headed for my desk. The one benefit of our respite from cases had been not nearly dying with her at the wheel. As a dragon-shifter, she didn't have to worry, nor did David. Finn and I were just witches, human, and not immortal.

My go bag still had a *Supernatural* patch on it, but David hadn't ribbed me about it, yet. We were going to travel through dinner time. Gratefully, I had snacks. Those and not watching the road would get me through Marie's driving.

Once we were on the team's little jet plane, Finn walked me through what he knew of the instances of Mahakala's quartz use. They were questionable, considering the passage of time.

I faced him in our quad of comfortable seats. My bottle of water was empty, drained during my mild anxiety of taking off. The craft did not seem as small as it had when I first flew in it.

"What do we know about the use of Earth magic?" I asked.

Finn chuckled. "More than you'll learn on a flight to Tallahassee. Broadly, it is very focused on organics. Dur-Alf and Mer realms yield forces: crush, bind, lock, unlock, etc. The Earth realm is used in Dur-Alf and Mer realms to heal or destroy organics."

I glanced to see if Marie might comment from a dragon-shifter's point of view.

Finn turned his eyes down. "Have you looked at the police reports?"

"Skimpy," I said.

He opened his folder and plucked at the pages incredulously. "Three witnesses?" Finn sounded frustrated. "Why just three? That doesn't make sense in a city the size of Tallahassee."

David stretched from where he sat across the aisle from me. "Lunchtime. Everybody inside getting a little nosh."

Finn frowned. "There's a deli near this corner. One of the witnesses had just bought his lunch there. Xavier Vasquez."

Tomas spoke over the comms. "You've got the one traffic cam. Nothing from it except the Volvo and a man in a cowboy hat crossing the street who never glances back."

Marie didn't look up from her phone. "Maybe one of the witnesses saw someone."

Finn flipped through pages. "The driver, Dan Norton, sees no one except the victim crossing the sidewalk. Then he spots the lady at the mailbox, Emily Brown. Xavier Vasquez doesn't show up until Dan's getting out of the car. Emily's worried about the victim's language and the littering. Xavier freaks out when he realizes the degree of damage to the mangled body. He does mention the other two witnesses."

"How far can an Earth realm spell be thrown?" I asked. David's suggestion that we were dealing with a dwarf or merfolk bothered me.

Marie still didn't look up. "Ranges vary between practitioner and spell. How far can you throw a binding spell?"

I shrugged. "Well, I've not really measured it."

Tomas coughed. "Kelsey Brigham estimated one hundred and fifty yards, 1931, in Mesa, Arizona. Longest we have recorded and witnessed."

I was still a bit infatuated with him, on a purely physical level, though I hadn't seen him but one time. "Tomas, how about an Earth realm spell which could crush bones? How far could that reach?" We might be talking a block and a half if it could be used the same distance as a binding spell.

"How the hell should I know?" The slight inhale at the end of his shout preceded an angrier comment. "You think this is a merfolk? You want me to ask my people?"

Marie turned her head up and shook it slowly.

"No. Well — sorry." I glanced from Finn to Marie. I had missed something which might cue me in to his moods. They weren't offering anything with the comms open.

He swore. "You are sorry." Tomas's tone was sharp and dripped with sarcasm.

I winced and looked down at my papers. This was not like his usual jabs; I'd mistakenly hit a soft spot with Tomas. Saying anything else might make it worse, so I kept quiet.

Marie's question snapped into the silence. "Tomas, is Stacey doing anything to clear up this Investigator Dee's bullshit?" She put her cell on her lap without glancing at the screen.

"Would you like me to tap into her phone?" he asked in a cold manner that made me wonder if he would.

"Your opinion would likely yield more."

"I think she's waiting for you to arrive and deal with it." Tomas spoke in a quiet tone, as if he hadn't been furious a minute before.

The Consociation had been a near mystical whisper in coven circles. We knew it was there. Verbal decrees had been passed down from over a century ago regarding penalties for those who still tempted fate and worked with Tarus. I hadn't expected that an executive department, such as we were, would have internal conflicts and politics.

"Perhaps," started David with a theatrical pause,

"Detective Dee will be persuaded by my overwhelmingly dashing charms."

"Investigator, not Detective. I might resort to having you flash him some fang." Marie sighed, appearing to relax.

I smiled a little at the thought, though I would have been mortified if she were serious. David noticed and rattled his mints at me.

The sun had dropped to mid-afternoon by the time we landed. The air smelled fresher, more like Grand Junction than Atlanta. I'd never been to Tallahassee before. The local FBI met us outside a small building that served private jets. The two men who dropped off the black SUV couldn't seem to leave quick enough.

Finn took a while organizing the back of the vehicle with our go bags and his rifle among the Kevlar vests provided by the local FBI. He ended up in the back with me again for his efforts. "Investigator Dee first?" he asked Marie as he buckled his seat belt.

"Meeting us at the scene." We raced along the winding airport road.

I focused on my water bottle. Our comms had been off since the end of the flight. "Do you think this could be a merfolk or dwarf?" I asked.

"They've been known to stray from accepted behavior. In recent times, murder has been rare. Both races have strict guidelines for entering the Earth realm." Finn's face tightened, his usual smile gone. "Tomas made some difficult decisions while his sister was sick. He ended up exiled when he married a human."

Marie tilted her head back to speak. "It is not something he would appreciate talking about. However, it is a good example of a non-humans rejecting the constraints of their realm's traditions and laws."

I sipped at my water. In my covens, we rarely ever talked about merfolk or dwarves. Tomas wore a wedding ring, but I never would have guessed it cost him exile from his own realm. What had happened to his sister? I wasn't about to push for more information and certainly wouldn't talk to Tomas about it.

David had called the dwarves nasty, and Finn had mentioned Herta disliked vampires. There were enough hints at animosity between the groups and the possible renegade behaviors that the use of the Earth realm by a non-human rose in my list of possibilities.

"Is it feasible some human is using an arcane ritual, or a witch has learned to cast a spell with the Earth realm?" I asked the question absently to the group rather than anyone specifically.

"Possible," Finn said. "However, unlikely."

When we drove down Monroe to the intersection, Marie passed through without taking any of the open parking spaces. I recognized the planters and two-story brick building at the corner from the crime scene photos.

A young, white man with a buzz cut of dark hair was scowling by a mailbox. He wore a black or dark blue uniform with a matching tie. A badge and stripes marked him as an officer.

"Detective Jimmy D, I presume." David watched the man through the tinted windows.

"Inspector," Marie corrected again as we passed a small park nestled as a median between east and west-bound Park Avenue. Few people appeared interested in using it.

David looked at Marie and mimicked a serious expression. "Pyre, I think we passed him."

"No shit." She turned left on Park Avenue, and we

circled the full block. "One of the witnesses said he threw a coffee into the planters."

"Littered and splattered everywhere," David added.

"She did say that." Marie slowly turned the corner at a hotel, heading back toward the intersection where the investigator waited. "Tomas, please find me local coffee. West of the scene."

"I'd prefer wine at this time of the day." David rattled mints over his shoulder.

"Where was he coming from? Where was he going?" Marie turned right onto Monroe Street, and we approached the investigator again. "I want to retrace his steps the morning before he died. Finn, David, you two hit up his office and hope someone's working late. Kristen and I will talk with Investigator Dee."

David appeared surprised. "I thought you needed me?" He opened his mouth, exposing the slightly elongated and sharp cuspids.

Marie turned the SUV off. "I don't trust you. You're in a mood."

He snorted, "My way of dealing with loss. I'll show you a picture of Alexandria, and you'll understand."

"Move it." She opened her door as I flung my belt off and scrambled for the door handle. "Comms."

I slapped my ear a little too hard.

Traffic was flowing down Monroe Street, mainly toward the intersection where Wendall had died. Exhaust hung in the air. Quieter than Atlanta, noise still filled the downtown road. Four lanes separated a mix of newer concrete, steel, and glass structures from older ones of brick and iron.

The uniformed man watched us pile out, studying each of us. As Marie locked eyes with him, she spoke to Tomas. "Any change?"

His voice pitched higher than usual, almost squeaked, at the first word, then dropped. "None. They've got the body locked down."

Marie strode onto the sidewalk. "Stacey?"

"Left for the day."

I swore Marie growled. I felt the rumble more in my feet than my ears. "Investigator Dee. Thank you for meeting us. This is the scene?"

He took his time speaking as he studied her bald head. "SSA Pyre?"

She nodded and pointed to me. "Agent Winters." Ignoring his inscrutable expression, she gestured to the crosswalk. "Here?" The stain was obvious.

"What department are you with? What is the DRC?" He eyed us suspiciously, in turn, with each question.

"Risk Containment. Is there a problem? You have released the body, haven't you?" Marie appeared concerned, as though she didn't know he stonewalled us.

Dee's chin jutted forward as his jaw tightened. "We're processing the forms. I'm going to need to know what's going on here." He threw the second comment in as if a threat to the first.

Marie ignored him and tapped her comms. "Tomas, how much time do we have before we need to bring in the CDC? Never mind, get hold of that Gibson, Major Gibson."

Stifling a smile, I sensed the investigator's panic as his face blanched. The emotion had to be strong to get through to my weak empath skills.

"No. I can work out the paperwork. I just . . ." He composed himself, and a wash of anger flushed pale cheeks. "No need to disturb Major Gibson. I'll work out the paperwork."

"Starbucks and a breakfast restaurant serve coffee. I'll

send links to your email." Tomas seemed undisturbed by her ruse and indifferent to our present conversation with the inspector.

"Tomas, hold that." Marie raised her eyebrows. "Are you sure, Investigator Dee? Now?"

Investigator Dee paused, perhaps trying to gauge or resist the situation. I studied the planters and found the cup from Starbucks. Casually, I strolled over and stuck two fingers inside, careful not to touch the outside.

"Fine." He spit out the word. "Keep my supervisor out of it. I'll be your liaison, though."

Marie didn't answer, and as I returned, the investigator pulled out his phone. His face stone, he scrolled across his screen. If he didn't scowl so much, he might have been handsome in a boyish way.

As Marie waited patiently and Dee focused on his cell, I took the cup to the SUV and put it under the seat where I'd stashed my purse.

"We're clear on the body, Pyre." Tomas spoke smoothly. "I'll get you an ETA and alert Udy."

I approached Marie, but she already had begun her disengagement with Dee, thanking him when she likely wanted to curse him. I glanced in the direction Finn and David had gone, across the street, but they were still inside. I reached Marie as the investigator strode away.

"Dancing monkeys. The males of your species can be intolerable." She glanced at me, as if to gauge my reaction. "I guessed that Investigator Dee kept a tight grip because of some ambition, once I saw how young he was. The only thing I had to do was threaten his shining record, and he crumpled. What a waste of time." Marie marched toward the stain in the crosswalk, studying the asphalt and brick.

Standing in the middle of the lane, she slowly turned,

peering at the buildings, windows, and balconies. "What did you do, Wendall Landon?"

I stood safely on the sidewalk, glancing where she did. My inexperience still hampered me. Tomas was building a database of information about our victim, but he hadn't sent a report yet. I'd study that as soon as we had a free moment.

Marie marched up to me. "What's next?"

I blinked. "Interview the three witnesses. Unless Finn and David come back with something."

She gestured toward the car and led the way. As I opened the car door, my phone vibrated.

CHAPTER

THREE

J ade was calling. My eyes widened. Finn and David were still inside the building. We would be waiting a minute, so I had time. I stepped away from the SUV and answered instead of getting in the car.

"Hi Honey. What's up? I'm sorry, I'm working." She might expect I should be getting home or miscalculated the time change. However, I couldn't remember the last time she'd called me.

"Are you okay?" Her voice was tight, panicked.

I turned off my comms. "I'm fine." She'd had one of her visions. I swallowed, my pulse rising. "What did you see?" I said quietly.

She sniffled and my heart wrenched. I wanted to be there comforting her, but we weren't like that, not since I left. Jade stammered. "I saw you — you were screaming in pain. I couldn't see what. It was gray, like Tarus. Like you'd been dragged there, and they were hurting you."

"I'm not, though. In fact, I'm in Florida. Tallahassee. Nothing to do with Tarus."

"You need to change something. Quit your job. Anything to make the vision not happen." Jade broke into sobs.

My chest was empty and tight at the same time. I struggled to breathe. "I'm fine. I'll be careful." I'd caused my daughter's panic. My ex, Anthony, would be furious.

Between breaths, she spoke in choppy fragments. "If you don't change something major, it'll happen. You know I'm right."

David swaggered out of the building, saw me on the phone, and reached into his top pocket. He waved a piece of paper at me. Finn followed, peering at traffic so they could cross.

"Honey, I've got to go. I'll call. Hopefully tonight."

"Mom." She only said the one word.

"I'll be careful."

"It won't be enough." She hung up and left me in silence.

As they jogged across the street, David kept the paper in the air. "Lindsey. Let's hope we have to stay the night."

I ignored him and headed for my door. Marie started the engine, and I pushed down the gloom and climbed into my seat. Jade's predictions often came true, but I hated that she had to live with such a horrid vision of my future. I knew I wouldn't leave Pyre's Pups though, and I'd failed Jade in that. It would have been some hint of hope for her if I agreed to do that one thing. Perhaps her warning was enough to keep her vision from becoming a reality.

Anthony would be livid; he and I had fought over Jade's ability. He refused to let some of the elder coven members help guide her. I couldn't decide what was best for her, but I didn't think isolation and ignoring it was the answer.

David bounced into his seat, slamming the door. "Lindsey. Taller than Finn, if I were to guess."

I could hear Marie's frown in her voice. "Stow it. What did you get?"

Finn closed his door. "Wendall had three clients in the morning. I've sent the list to Tomas along with the person he was supposed to meet at noon. He often goes and gets lunch near Starbucks, grabs a coffee, and walks back to pitch midday clients who use their lunch hour to meet with him. Nothing unusual today, except that he didn't show up for his noon meeting. Local police questioned the secretary over the phone."

Marie backed into the road with a jerk. "This Lindsey?"

"No. Veronica Smithers. Lindsey sells insurance in the office next to Wendall's."

We lurched down Monroe Street. "Tomas, dig deep."

I tapped my comms back on when I didn't hear his response.

". . . employment records from the IRS and will do the same on the egg place and Starbucks."

"Thanks." Marie yanked us sharply to the left. "Tomas, call Dan Norton, let's see if we can interview the driver first. I'm heading toward his residence until you get me an alternate location."

Ten minutes later we stood outside a steak restaurant with the scent of grilling meat wafting in the air. Our witness had agreed to meet us outside.

He stepped toward us hesitantly from the front door. Dan Norton was a reserved man in his forties with an even tan that appeared to have come from a salon. He wore a pastel yellow polo and blue slacks.

As we talked, Finn tugged at the Mer realm, perhaps searching for illusions. I hadn't even thought of it.

The witness tapped the edge of his phone with his fingers as he related the event. "I don't know what he was yelling, but he seemed furious, and after he gave me the finger, I thought he had a heart attack or stroke. The man just dropped into the street. Never moved, that I could see." Dan grimaced. "His body — it looked wrong. Limp with bones sticking out." He shivered. "Then the Mexican guy came running over and started praying."

"American, born in Colorado," Marie corrected. "Who else saw Mr. Landon fall?"

"The mousy chick on the sidewalk. Then a guy in a truck pulls up and just parks there so I can't even pull out of the intersection. No one wanted to touch the guy on the ground. I mean, *really* creepy."

Marie squinted lightly. "Anyone else? The woman and the two men?"

Dan shrugged. "Sure, more people stood on the side-walk by the time the police showed up. I told the cops what I knew. Why is the FBI interested in this? A terrorist or something?"

"You don't know any of them?" she asked. "The other people who gathered?"

Dan snorted. "No. I wouldn't have been in that part of town if it weren't for a chiropractor appointment."

Marie studied the man for a moment, then handed him a card. "Leave me a message if you think of anyone else who witnessed the man falling."

Dan took the card and quickly headed back inside the restaurant. I gave the establishment a longing look and promised myself a protein bar during our drive to see the other witnesses. From their statements, they knew each other and even lived in the same apartment complex.

I followed the team to the SUV, itching to call Jade back just to try and reassure her.

"It's not looking like we're coming up with anything new." Finn walked beside Marie.

"Let's see if the other two have anything to add." She sighed. "If not, we'll spend the night and canvas the egg restaurant employees to find out if anything strange happened during his early lunch."

David turned toward me with an exaggerated grin which showed his fangs, waving Lindsey's number.

"Stow it," Marie said, without glancing back at us.

Giggling, David entered the number into his phone and began texting.

As we pulled out of the restaurant parking lot, Tomas confirmed that Xavier hadn't answered his calls. "He's got some minor priors for fighting, but they're all over ten years ago."

While it was still full afternoon, we sped through back roads just off Park Avenue to the apartment complex where both Xavier Vasquez and Emily Brown lived. The street turned slow and shaded as it led to a more residential area a short distance away. We drove over a small bridge shading old railroad tracks surrounded by towering trees.

Down a short side street, we turned into the drive of their apartments. The large, two-story structures needed as much repair as the cars in the parking lot. I'd lived in similar circumstances when I first joined the Grand Junction police department. Kids were tossing a basketball at the end of the drive while a couple of tenants smoked in the short swales of grass. The balconies circled central lawns visible from the parking spaces.

No one answered the second-floor apartment where Xavier Vasquez lived alone, so we headed for Emily Brown's. The cozy courtyard had a narrow view of the parking lot from the lower level.

David lifted his head up, sniffing in a deep breath.

"Lovely." Someone had been smoking pungent marijuana, but our presence seemed to have had a quieting effect on the community. We all wore suits, so it wasn't surprising. David returned to his incessant texting and giggled as we walked.

The front of Emily's apartment had a number of dead orchids in hangers and a bright ceramic frog, which I liked. The worn doormat offered a Merry Christmas, either four months late or way too early. Classical music sounded from the other side of the door.

"Hmm. Brahms," David said. His tone didn't offer a hint if he approved or not.

Marie rapped on the door firmly. Tomas had called to confirm Emily was home.

A thud came from inside, then the music stopped. The woman who opened the door had red puffy eyes from crying and wore a blue robe and a long black T-shirt over yoga pants.

"Emily Brown?" Marie asked.

The blue-green Mer realm shifted as Finn tugged at it to test for wards. I pursed my lips and shoved down self-doubts. We would need to search for illusions, at least on this case. I would learn.

The woman nodded solemnly and stepped back, allowing us into her apartment. Marie introduced us all, but I doubted Emily even heard our names. The coffee table held wadded tissues, a box of fresh ones, and a partial tray of peanut butter cookies.

"Are you okay?" I asked.

She rubbed her face, but the question seemed to soften her mood. "I'll be alright. Rough couple weeks. Sit, sit." She frowned when David settled his jacket and his holster showed.

The seating she offered was a beige couch that might fit three, or just me and Marie comfortably. The only other seat was a black stool under a folding stand supporting an electric keyboard.

I dismissed her offer to sit with a wave. "I've been sitting in a car all day."

Emily turned and walked toward the kitchen off to the right. "Does everyone like sweet tea?"

Marie frowned and Finn grinned, tilting his head. "I love sweet tea. Let me help." He strode after Emily.

David tapped at the silent keyboard. Gratefully, it wasn't on. He slid out the stool and sat, still focused on the instrument. Marie paced the room, finally sitting on the end of the couch. From our discussion, we didn't have another interview planned for today, unless we could find Xavier.

With glasses rattling and Finn talking with Emily, I pointed to the tissues. "I think she's upset about the incident."

Marie nodded sharply. "Likely."

David had powered up the electric keyboard and tapped out a couple notes, adjusting the knobs. Marie said nothing, but I glanced over to the kitchen. It seemed rude.

The delicate melody he played echoed lightly in the room but sounded as if he sat at a piano. Clearly classical, I had no idea who the composer might be.

His fingers flowed smoothly over the instrument, and the music danced around us. I had a difficult time connecting the mastery of the composition to my vampire teammate. David's skill awed me.

From the kitchen, Finn peeked around the doorway and shook his head. Marie snorted. "Stow it, David."

The music stopped and he turned with his broad handsome grin. He appraised my expression. "I had a crush on a voluptuous brunette named Deirdre."

I doubted that was the full truth and turned away to hide my smile.

When Finn and a stiff-faced Emily returned with full glasses, David stood up and offered the stool. "Would you play us something?" he asked with a flourish.

She studied the table as she leaned to place two glasses of iced tea. "I'm in no mood. I'm out of work, and some heartless bastard killed my dog."

I frowned. "Your dog? That's horrible. Why? How?"

Finn handed me a glass.

"Two days ago. Some uncaring girl just raced down the street when Rascal and I were crossing it." Emily paused, her voice tightening. "She never stopped. Never looked." Her face screwed tight as if she might cry, then she drew in a long breath. "I lost my remote job a week ago — and had been walking my baby a lot those past few days. The fresh air helps me think." She wrung her hands after she placed our drinks. "Xavier talked me into going for lunch today, and . . ."

As Emily paused, Marie interrupted. "Xavier. We've been trying to contact him. Do you know where he is?"

Emily's forehead wrinkled. "He should be going to work soon. He works the late shift."

David waved away Finn's offer of sweet tea. I sipped, appearing to enjoy the powdered mix taste. We had to keep Emily calm if we expected any answers.

"I have to ask about today." Marie softened her tone. "We have your report about the deceased yelling at people, the car honking, and the coffee spilling on you."

"Left a stain." Her face tightened angrily. "Foul language. Nobody should act like that." Emily calmed and shrugged. "I only paid attention to Xavier. We normally go together for lunch on Tuesdays because Xavier has the late shift. I go every day. They have good pastrami. Except I missed a day last week because my cousin Dale is in town and we drove to Quitman, in Georgia. He's a picker. Dale is. Digs up things in old dumps he calls middens. Says this area's gold for picking if you find someone selling out of their old barn. He drove down in a U-Haul."

Marie sighed. "So, no other people were present when the man fell?"

Emily shook her head. "Xavier dropped our lunch, not that I felt like eating afterward."

We were getting nowhere with her rambling. If she worked remotely, she might be lonely and just want to talk. Perhaps more so since she was out of work. Personally, I might have cut back on lunches out, but I didn't know her finances and wasn't about to bring it up.

"I'm so sorry to hear about your dog, Rascal. I can't imagine being without my baby." I lied easily, since I had lost pets before I'd joined the force. "What breed?"

"Purebred mongrel." Emily smiled weakly. "Do you want to see her picture?"

"I'd love to." I nodded and cooed over her phone for a moment, both Marie and Finn watching me patiently. "Before she was killed, did you bring Rascal to the deli when you walked there?"

Emily slowly shook her head. "Too busy and loud."

I circled into the question I had wanted to ask. "You said the deceased was yelling at people. Can you describe them?"

She frowned. "A man. He had on a hat — maybe a Stetson?"

"Was he yelling back? Did you see his face?"

Emily's expression pinched tight. "No, he was walking across the street."

"Park Avenue?" I asked.

She nodded, stretching her fingers and studying them.

Marie stood and produced a card. "If you remember anyone else in the vicinity when the man fell, please call and leave me a message."

Emily took the card and began twisting it. "Okay. Sorry I couldn't be more help." Her expression soured when she noted Marie's untouched tea. I quickly finished mine.

David opened the front door, and Emily tsked, crossing the room to turn her instrument off. Marie gave him a light glare and followed him out.

Finn pointed toward the kitchen with his empty glass. "Should we leave these in the kitchen? Delicious tea."

She frowned and shook her head, taking his glass. "I'll take care of it."

When she reached for mine, I smiled. "Thank you. Very kind of you."

She smiled faintly and took our glasses. "No bother. I've got nothing else to do." Her lips tightened. "I hope you find what you're looking for." Emily hadn't asked us why we were investigating.

Marie and Pyre were already nearing the sidewalk as Emily stepped out. "Oh, there's Xavier." Her tone certainly brightened. She likely had a slight crush.

In his mid-thirties with a warm brown complexion, Xavier had short black hair and wore a tan work shirt and jeans. He jingled keys as he quickly strode across the parking lot toward a silver Dodge sedan.

"Xavier Vasquez," Marie called as she veered across the grass in his direction. David trotted behind her.

With a quizzical expression, the man peered at us but shook his head. "I'm late for work," he called back, never breaking his stride.

David and Pyre jogged to catch him before he got in his car. "FBI," she said. "We need to talk with you."

"I'm late." He waved her off and was obviously not pausing for them. His expression hadn't changed at the mention of the FBI; perhaps he hadn't heard her.

"Stop!" yelled Marie, her tone losing patience.

Finn had remained with Emily, so I followed suit. Clenching our empty glasses in a white-knuckled grip, she stepped to the edge of the concrete.

"He can't be late," Emily explained. "They might fire him."

Marie began to run as Xavier reached his car and opened his door. She was a good twelve yards away. He showed no intention of waiting for them.

I tensed. He might be late for work, or a dwarf in disguise. David could have reached him by now, if he chose to expose his unnatural speed.

"What are they doing?" Emily's pitch rose, and I dimly sensed her stress rise.

"It's okay," I said. "They just want to talk with him." Resting my hand on her arm, I tried to calm her.

Xavier's car door slammed, and the engine started.

"He'll be late." Emily was adamant, her tone rising to anger.

David alongside her, Marie slowed her pace. "Xavier Vasquez, turn off the vehicle and step out. This is an FBI investigation, and you will comply."

The local kids had stopped to watch the ruckus. A door opened from one of the apartments above. A smoker stepped to the railing on the second floor near us and flicked his ashes.

As Xavier punched his car into reverse, Marie spun away, abandoning her pursuit. Positioned two parking spaces away, she gestured to our SUV. "Move it. We'll catch him at his job."

Finn and I both shifted, preparing to leave Emily fretting.

David matched Marie's turn, then faltered. His leg twisted.

Xavier's tires chirped.

Mid-step, Marie collapsed. Her face slapped against the asphalt. Her body jiggled with the impact. At her thigh, a spike poked her pants up into a small tent.

When David fell behind her, he stumbled sideways, screaming before reaching out to break his fall.

"Not again," whispered Emily in a horrified voice. Glass and ice shattered on her step, but I was already running with Finn.

David lay motionless with a second bend in his jacket sleeve. Faced away from us, his scream had become a groan, then stopped.

Marie hadn't moved since her initial fall, but as we raced across the parking lot, her eyes followed our movement. Chills rolled up my shoulders and neck.

Xavier never slowed, speeding around the curve and behind other apartment buildings. My focus burned on the back of his car for a moment before turning back to my team. David couldn't be dead, as it took severing of a vampire's head or burning, from what little I'd been told. Marie wasn't really here, or at least not all of her. I wasn't sure what could be done to her.

Long-legged Finn reached her first, and he bent down as if to touch her or roll her over. A wave of emotion slammed into me. Finn flinched back. I suddenly knew I wouldn't lay a finger on Marie. She couldn't be touched.

Marie must have hit us both with a type of compulsion, because for a moment, little churned in my mind except the overwhelming desire not to disturb her. I slowed, jogging the last few paces. My pulse raced.

"Xavier?" Finn asked, but more to himself than to me or Marie. "Did he do this?"

Peering at Marie's wide eyes, I shivered. "Well, I think so."

FOUR

The world around me shrank as my vision tunneled on Marie and David lying crippled on the asphalt. I started when Tomas spoke over the comms. "Pyre? What happened?"

Finn swallowed. "Pyre and David are down. They've been hit with the same effect as our victim. Call for transport or get Herta to us."

Blood soaked Marie's suit at her thigh and seeped into the asphalt. Her skin had blotches of angry red, already leaning toward purple.

Emily's sobbing voice sounded across the parking lot. "Not again."

Running footsteps scuffed from another direction, and I experienced another wave of compulsion, but I knew it for what it was now. I snapped back into focus and gazed around us. The complex had come alive with people. Phones were out and taking videos. Emily shuffled toward us.

"Get rid of her," whispered Finn in a tone as close to anger as I'd heard from him.

Gesturing back toward the apartments, I yelled out to her. "Call the paramedics." Likely someone had already, but Tomas would deal with it all.

"Catch Xavier," David spoke with a squelch from two paces away.

Circling a wide berth around Marie, I approached him. Bones pushed through various locations in his arms and legs, protruding into his fine suit. He would hate the way the blood ruined his pants and pooled at his shoe. His skin had the same dark red and purple blotches spreading across his jaw and cheek.

"You can speak," I said. A foolish comment, but I was stunned and scared for them both.

His handsome face had gone wrong at the jaw; muscles barely moved as he spoke. "No pain." He wet his lips. "Marie?"

"Alive." I crouched, focusing on his eyes rather than his ruined body. "What can I do?" I realized my mistake as his lips shifted, trying to smile.

His lip peeled up, revealing a cuspid. "Thirsty."

"You didn't finish your tea." I wanted to reassure him, but assumed his strange Tarus chemistry was working to heal him. Truthfully, in this situation, I didn't have any idea what I should do. "Tomas, is there something I should be doing for Marie or David?"

"Herta is coordinating with one of our medical teams now. Keep them safe. I would suggest not touching them."

"Catch Xavier," David repeated slowly.

Finn joined me. "We're not leaving until we've got transport." His voice was firm, and he spoke to David and me in turn. "We need something from the archives before we approach Xavier. There's a talisman, Yan's Pin, a vampire artifact from a darker time in our history. It'll protect a human against Earth realm magic, but it has to pierce the skin."

I studied him. "Which you'll wear. While I'm off somewhere being safe, I assume."

He nodded. "It's my command until Pyre is back on her feet." A wince rolled across his expression. "I have to check in with Stacey. Tomas, send her a preliminary report and let her know I'll call once we have transport here."

"I already sent it." Tomas swore. "I'll update her on when she can expect a call."

I searched the area around us; most of the tenants stuck to the grassed area or sidewalk, keeping their distance. Emily had gone into her apartment.

"Go probe Emily for more information on Xavier. We're looking for any indication that he's not human or wears a quartz crystal. Don't push too hard."

Watching her door, I tugged at my curls. "What if it's her?"

Finn shook his head. "We know she's not a dwarf, and I touched her, so did you. She's not from another realm."

"Meaning she's not merfolk." Tomas cut in, saying the name of his people like a curse.

Smiling apologetically, Finn continued, "She's wearing a robe, yoga pants, and a thin T-shirt. Where would she be hiding Mahakala's quartz? I don't think so. Wouldn't we all be in the same condition?"

"You said it affected enemies. Maybe she didn't see us that way. Only . . ." I turned toward Marie. She lay there, unmoving.

He tilted his head toward her apartment. "Then be careful, and be polite."

Giving David a glance, I nodded and headed for Emily. My knowledge of dragon-shifters I could write in the palm of my hand. Myths and legends abounded, but if they were true, she would have faded back to Salmhalla and returned renewed. Maybe Finn knew more. I had never searched Tomas's database on that subject. When I reached the sidewalk, Emily came out of her door with a dustpan and brush.

"Did you call?" I asked, following up on my pretext to have her clear out of the area.

"They're coming. Are they — okay?"

I stood just off her stoop. "I think they will be."

She nodded, then crouched to scoop up the broken glass and ice. "Xavier hasn't done anything wrong."

"I'll convince them of that. Tell me about him. Did you meet here?"

Emily paused and darted a glance at me, suspicious. "Why?"

A chill ran up my spine and I imagined melting here on the concrete walkway. No, Jade had seen me in pain in Tarus. I wouldn't die here. "I don't want them wasting their time with Xavier."

Even with my lame explanation, she filled her dustpan with sharp, frustrated sweeps. "What do you want to know?" Her tone was sharp and her speech quick.

"How long have you known him?" I didn't know the questions to out a non-human.

Emily left the pan on her stoop and crossed her arms. "I don't know. A couple years. He was here when I moved in."

"Is he normally that stressed? Like he was today?"

She sniffed. "Your boss was going to make him late."

I was over my head. "Tell me some things about him. What kind of sandwiches does he like when you go to the deli? Things like that."

"This is ridiculous. He's a considerate man. Italian subs."

"Not merfolk," said Tomas over the comms.

Emily waved her hands in the air, and I flinched. "This is just a witch hunt. He's done nothing. What is it you people are accusing him of?"

"Nothing," I said. "Nothing." No matter what Finn said, I did not want to be this woman's enemy. "I think I've got enough to convince them." I smiled through my frustration.

She shoved her hands in her robe and twitched her head. "I'm not convinced." Emily pulled her hand out of her pocket and pointed at Marie. "She was going to chase him."

"She's not going to, and we're not going to." I raised my hands, trying to calm her. My bones still felt intact. Perhaps Finn was right. "I'm sorry to get you upset. If you remember anyone else from today, please call us."

Emily drooped. "I'm sorry. I'm sorry your friends are hurt. It's been a difficult week."

"I understand. It's difficult to lose your dog. I know what it's like to lose a pet." Actually, I'd left my cat with my ex. Fighting to become a detective had taken all my time. I waved goodbye and took a deep breath as I headed back toward Finn.

"Tomas, why would eating an Italian sub mean he's not merfolk?"

He swore. "Are you illiterate? Don't you even look at the database? We don't eat mammals. We'd get sick."

Sagging, I locked eyes with Marie. She appeared alert, but still not showing a hint of movement.

"Tomas, how long will it take Marie to heal?"

"A few days."

"And David?"

"The same. Quicker with human blood."

No matter what Emily thought, it was probably Xavier.

I would have been a puddle if she had the ability. If Finn felt it best to use the talisman, then I would fight to be nearby.

It took twenty minutes before four paramedics pulled up in two standard emergency vehicles with Tallahassee clearly written on the sides. If Tomas had not warned us they were pulling into the complex, I would have thought them regular EMTs.

When they leaned down to put Marie on the collapsed gurney, streams from the Mer realm cocooned my boss. Bones shifted under her clothes, and blood dripped.

With David, they appeared to be a little less careful. His arm looked odd, even as they shifted it onto his stomach. Lying face up, he caught my eye, and his lips moved. I stepped over to him.

"Don't forget—" he wet his lips "—to donate." His jaw barely moved as he talked.

I frowned. "What?"

"Bloodmobile."

I groaned, then leaned in. "Hang in there. B positive."

David's lips tried to curl at the edges into a smile, then he coughed and the medics slid him into the van.

Finn stood looking at the two blood stains. I joined him. "How can they survive, losing this much blood?"

Finn tilted his head. "You're assuming a different physiology. Vampires have been completely drained and gone dormant, regenerating within a week. They'll be okay, eventually. David will heal quicker, but he won't be at peak health for a while. I've seen Pyre take a few bullets and spells. Two of them were meant for me. She's tough, but this is different."

I had no energy after the two vehicles drove away. Hunger gnawed at me, and that just brought up guilt. "We should go after Xavier." I didn't want him causing damage to someone else, but the options didn't seem good unless Finn put a bullet in the man. I couldn't be sure Xavier was the culprit. I studied the tenants gathered around.

"No." Finn gestured toward the SUV. "I'll drop you and the go bags at the hotel, then I fly back and pick up Yan's Pin." He walked toward the vehicle, and I kept pace. "When I get back, we'll go after Xavier. You can get a couple hours sleep. You'll be watching my six when I approach him in case something goes bad."

"I'll go with you."

Finn shook his head. "Tomas, where's Xavier?"

It took a moment before Tomas cursed. "I'm intercepting calls to the local police department and scrubbing social media for images of Pyre and David. I missed Xavier turning off his phone. Twelve minutes ago. I don't know where he is."

Finn's eyebrows lifted, and he mouthed "missed" before he spoke. "That's okay. Wouldn't have mattered. We aren't going to approach him unprotected. Where was he when he shut off his cell?"

"His job. You have the coordinates. Remember, Stacey is waiting on your call."

Groaning, Finn dug for his cell. I wondered how she'd react to him being in command. Did that change things? Some superiors wanted to take over the case if they lost their lead. What would that be like, working for Stacey?

"Tomas, what's Herta's plan?" Finn sounded concerned. "If she's flying them back, I need to be on that plane."

"Ground. Herta and Udy are on an intercept; she wants to do some preliminary work as soon as possible."

We reached the car, and it felt odd getting in the front seat. Finn stopped at the back and grabbed some water.

I didn't want to stay while he flew back and forth to

Atlanta. Even after I ate, I doubted I'd sleep. Buckling into my seat, I tried to work up a good argument.

"Tomas, have local police check Xavier's work for his car. Can you please call his job, see if he's left?" Finn climbed in, handed me a water, and tapped his phone. I'd have to wait until he dealt with Stacey before I offered my argument.

"Billings, what's your situation?" Stacey's voice growled from his phone.

Finn started the car. "We've got a solid suspect, Xavier Vasquez. I'm heading back to pick up Yan's Pin. We've lost the cell trace, so I need an alert-only APB on him and his car."

We paused in the parking space, and I dreaded the idea Stacey might want to join us. Finn appeared as grim as me.

"How'd you lose the trace?"

"We believe he turned his cell off."

"The new witch, Winters, she wasn't tailing him?"

"No. We were at the scene." He tapped a finger on the steering wheel. "Didn't make sense to split, and I wanted to get as much out of the other witness to the original scene as possible."

"Bad call. Obviously, since we've lost our suspect. Check with me next time." The connection hung silent before we realized she'd hung up.

We sat with the quiet rumbling of the car engine before he tucked his phone away and put the SUV into reverse. Shadows covered the car from the trees; it would be night soon. "Tomas, please get the jet ready," Finn said.

The scent of mint reminded me that I was sitting in David's usual seat. "If an APB comes in tonight, I can't approach Xavier any more than a patrol car can." I began with my first series of logic as to why I should go back to Atlanta with Finn.

Finn wasn't listening and tapped on the steering wheel. "Gary wants me to retire. Open a bookstore. He's a witch, did I tell you?"

We passed the blood stains. Our audience had gone back to their apartments.

"No." It was a safe answer as I hadn't heard about any of this. No wonder Finn had been quiet lately. I understood the pressure family could put on us.

I couldn't help but raise my eyebrows at the red and green taco truck parked in the lot around the corner. Normally, I would have made a comment about it. They were here for the blood — David's at least.

"He doesn't know the details of what I do. You signed the same non-disclosure, but he's seen the wounds and figured most of it out. Werewolves leave a distinct mark."

I had the scars on my back. Waiting for him to continue, I twisted at my curls. He needed to talk about this.

"I'm considering it. I'd postponed any thoughts about it after Van's death." His dreads shifting, he shook his head as if arguing with his own mind. "It makes me cautious — with my own life and others. The problem is, any plans toward it bring out the same protective instinct, and I can't leave Pyre's Pups with you untrained. I have to make a decision soon."

His concern over my level of inexperience surprised me, though it shouldn't have. I showed how green I was with my ignorance. It would be months before I'd gotten through a single percent of Tomas's database. "I catch on quickly. We'd manage."

We pulled onto the main road, and he sighed. "Tomas, find us rooms, if you haven't already."

"Wait," I said. "I can't do anything here. I'm too wound up to sleep. Until you get back with this talisman, we're not doing anything. There's nothing we can do until Xavier pops back up, and he could be on I-10 heading west."

Tomas broke in at my comment. "He left work on a family emergency. His car is in the lot according to local enforcement. Let them impound it?"

Our trail was growing colder by the minute. "Yes," Finn said. "Check Emily Brown's calls and see if she warned him."

"Could they be working together?" I asked.

"I doubt it, but she's got a thing for the man. I can tell." He nodded to himself. "Map us to the airport. Tomas, hold on the rooms. We're going to get a night's rest unless Xavier triggers the APB. Otherwise, we return tomorrow, follow Pyre's trail, and find out what Wendall had been up to yesterday morning. I don't believe it'll yield anything new."

I released my breath silently and relaxed. Wendall wasn't our only victim now. As quickly as Xavier had vanished, he could be a dwarf. Part of me wanted to know that Herta had seen to Pyre and David and that they'd be okay. Directions populated my cell's map. "Turn left here at Franklin Boulevard."

Finn pulled up to the light. "I'll bring you to the Vault in the morning. Meet me at the office at seven."

"Okay." I shifted in my seat, recognizing the unease that came with a cooling case. Hunger gnawed at my stomach, rightfully so, but partly because I wanted to lean away from the feeling. What Xavier, if it was him, had done to people horrified me. I wouldn't be sleeping anytime soon. My go bag was in the back with our equipment. "What if it isn't Xavier?" I asked.

"Then we're going to be questioning everyone in the complex. Their apartments weren't far from the corner where Wendall went down." Finn didn't appear pleased about his answer.

Twenty minutes later when we settled in our seats of the small jet plane, the two empty spaces left us silent. I had a protein bar and a small bag of cheddar crisps readied for the flight. Before we took off, I dialed Jade for a quick and public call. Hopefully, she had calmed down.

FIVE

Even with it nearly ten at night, I had Finn drive me back to my car. He had appeared introspective and thoughtful since his comment about retirement. His smile didn't have the same energy as I hefted my purse and go bag off the back seat. "Keep at it," he said.

I nodded at his homage to Marie. Xavier still seemed the best lead we had; however, it didn't mean he was our culprit.

Once back to my warm, stuffy car, I took time during the drive home to order pizza delivery. One good thing about Atlanta, you could get a meal anytime.

The day flashed through my mind, and the only thought I couldn't shake was Finn's comment on my inexperience. It was true, and not an insult. If he left, there would be someone new, and possibly as out of touch with the shadow world Pyre's Pups had to manage. I'd been in three covens, and not one had prepared me for this. Why would they? I still had not joined one of the hundreds of Atlanta covens. Recommendations and referrals had been made, but I hadn't followed up or visited anybody.

As witches, we used our magic quietly and privately. I had a skill with fast spells, but that hadn't been very useful except to pour myself a second cup of coffee while my hands were busy. The few times I'd tempted fate and used a realm for work, it had been when I knew most of the players. Now, when I needed my magic the most, I found myself lacking the knowledge that might make it useful.

Turning into my apartment complex, I pushed aside the day's issues and focused on home. I'd be happy for a shower and time to work on my character cards. I'd already sketched one for Finn as a warrior-mage, though he'd never see it. My collection often exposed more about me than my co-workers or friends. I'd scrapped three designs for Marie since I kept adding wings. Traffic was a breeze, and the parking lot at my apartment complex appeared asleep.

As I parked, a car pulled in behind me, and I shifted my mirror to peer at the occupants. Astrid's tall figure climbed out of the back, shouldering a backpack. She turned directly toward me and caught me watching. Flushing, I opened my door and waved to her. "You're out late," I said.

"Hiking. There's a Stone Mountain here in the city." Her driver pulled away, and she walked toward me. "How about you? Working late or having fun?" Under the dim lights, the blue and purple streaks barely showed their color in her blonde hair.

"Work." I didn't go into detail. The few times we passed each other on the stairs, she'd learned that I never talked about work. I hefted my purse and go bag, locked my doors, and let her lead the way to our stairs. "How was the hike?"

"Wonderful. There is some amazing and diverse flora

here. Most of the plants I've never seen." She stepped quickly, so soon after hiking. "I'm starving though."

I plodded under the weight of my go bag. "Me too." My cheeks flushed as I thought of my soon-to-be-delivered meal. "I've got pizza coming, if you want some."

Her head twitched, but she didn't pause or glance back. "Are you sure?"

"Of course. Let me change. Come on over in a couple minutes."

Astrid had reached the landing and turned to watch me. "I'd like that. We'll keep it short. I know you head out to work early. A quick chat over pizza would be nice."

Stumbling inside, I used the Mer realm to lift my go bag off my shoulder and tuck it on the kitchen counter. Pulling a second spell as I headed for the bedroom, I tossed my heavy purse onto the bed ahead of me and started to peel off clothes. I cast my sweaty bra aside, swiped my armpits with deodorant, and threw on sweats well before Astrid knocked.

I had napkins on the table and a list of available beverages inventoried from the fridge when I let her in.

Astrid stood tall with knobby joints. She too had donned fresh clothes, a plain pink T-shirt and jeans. "How close is this layout to yours?" I asked. The kitchen of my apartment led from the front door through an alcove dining area to the living room and the back patio. Bedrooms and the bath were through a door to the right.

She walked halfway into the dining area. "Heavens, you're neat. I'm glad we didn't eat at my apartment. I'm still scattered everywhere, and we moved in at the same time."

I got a little obsessive about having everything in the right place. Roommates in college had driven me nuts, as had my ex, Anthony. I was grateful Finn had similar traits since David was a slob and Marie a pack rat. My expression drooped as I thought of them. "A tour then."

My living room I kept sparse with a couch, an easy chair, a glass coffee table, and matching end tables. The television was new since I'd moved to Atlanta. Astrid gave it a cursory glance and pointed to my digital art, the only one of mine among three others. "I like that. A wizardess in her home glade."

My brow creased at her term. Most people just called my character a witch or sometimes sorceress. "Thank you."

Astrid turned to study me, cocking her head. "You made that?"

I always squirmed when it came to conversation about my art. Sometimes I liked my work, sometimes I didn't. Other people knowing it was my art seemed to put me in the position of being judged. I had to force myself to admit, "Yes."

"Very nice. You don't do that for the Federal government, art that is?"

I snorted. "No."

She pointed to the hall. "Do you have more?"

I led her to the left where I'd set up the second bedroom as my studio. Two desks formed the corner ahead to the left with my computer on one and my Wacom tablet on the other, though I had other peripherals. My stool and art table took up the right corner with shelving and supplies on every available wall that wouldn't block light or my closet.

Astrid strode directly for my art table where Finn was pinned on my board. "These are lovely. A male wizard with quite an impressive sword. How could he lift such a thing?"

I chuckled. "Let's say it's a magical weapon or he has magical strength. They're just fantasy character cards."

"Not a real person then?" Astrid leaned in, studying my work.

Well, yes. "Just a character."

The rap on the door saved me from a deeper lie.

The aroma leaked out of the pizza box as I got us drinks. While I wanted to stuff two slices into my mouth at once, Astrid ate sparingly, peppering me with questions. She grew used to waiting for me to chew between answers.

"Ontario, isn't that to the north? In a neighboring country?" She asked in an immediate response to my latest answer.

"The most famous Ontario is there. Where I grew up is in eastern Oregon. Very small town, if you would call it that." I started to take another bite and paused. "The country to the north is Canada." Who wouldn't know that? I knew nothing about Astrid. "Are you from the US?"

"Norway." She frowned slightly. "My parents were from the — America. You too are from America?" Astrid being from Norway might explain some of her oddness.

"Yes. Oregon is *in* the western US."

"You were from the police there?"

"Malheur County. Sheriff's Department." I had slowed, but still worked on my third slice of pizza.

Astrid nodded, seeming pleased with herself. "Next was detective."

"Next was Boise City Police." I took another bite to pause. Boise brought back memories of the long commutes and nights away from Jade, then the divorce and my failed attempt to have my daughter live with me. I would rather talk about after that time, when I'd grown used to being away from her. I spoke with my hand in front of my mouth, wanting to preempt her asking about Boise. "I didn't become detective until Grand Junction."

"Is it a nice place?" She finally took a bite, still working on her first slice.

"I liked it." If I were honest, I missed Yaz, our coven, and even my detective partner Greeley and his stupid obsession with his Irish roots.

The occasional drinks with Pyre's Pups and Finn's husband were the extent of my social engagement at the moment. Yaz had labeled me a loner, but I had often gone out with the other detectives to the bar. I was still settling in here in Atlanta. A few drinks with the team were enough for now.

"Why move here?"

We were back to my taboo topic, what I did for the federal government, where I didn't actually work. My pay came from the FBI, and I worked in their building, but that was it. "It's warmer. Maybe I'll go hiking someday. I grew up near the mountains and hiked with my dad and grandmother."

"Ontario?" Astrid asked. "Do you visit them?"

I had managed to shift Astrid off the topic of my work, but Leyn's death still hurt, six years later. My grandmother had been my strongest mentor in magic and life in general. "They died. My father when I was twelve, and my grandmother a few years ago." Forcing a smile, I tried to brighten the conversation. "I visit my mom and her new husband when I go out to see my daughter, Jade. I'm hoping to get out there this summer. Maybe we'll go hiking."

Astrid winced. "Sorry, I shouldn't have asked."

"It's fine." I pulled out another slice of pizza and waved it at her. "How about your family? Do you get to see them?"

Her smile was forced for the first time. "We're — rarely in contact. I travel too much."

Evidently it was my turn to bring out difficult memories. "I can understand. Tell me about the hike, what did you see?"

Astrid described the trees and scenery with amazing detail. I could see her passion there. We both were new to Atlanta, so we brought up places we'd heard of, yet not visited. My slice remained a crust on my plate as I listened to her describe her visit to a local botanical garden. She'd barely eaten through half her second slice before she suddenly decided it was time to go. I'd enjoyed talking with her, but my Norwegian neighbor certainly was odd.

I tucked away the leftovers and strolled through my apartment trying to determine whether I could sleep or not. Jumping on my computer, I tracked the amount of time it took to drive from Tallahassee to Atlanta. Marie and David would be halfway home. Herta might even be with them. When I woke in the morning, they'd be settled in — somewhere. Finn would brief me.

I moved to his card at the art table and sent streams of the Mer realm to retrieve two pens. I'd deal with Xavier and my team tomorrow.

CHAPTER

SIX

The office smelled like apples or pears when I arrived at 7:20 and found Finn already sitting at his desk.

He lifted his head and smiled, but not the broad grin he'd shown me yesterday morning. A lot had changed. "Stacey wants me to wait until she comes in so we can have a meeting. We're not heading to Tallahassee yet."

"Well, what time does she get in?" I resented her interference, partially because of her lack of support yesterday, though it wasn't her fault David and Marie were hurt.

His jaw tightened, then relaxed and he shrugged. "Later."

I stuffed my purse in my drawer and dropped my resupplied go bag by his at the file cabinets. "Marie? David?"

"Recuperating. Herta's doing the autopsy on Wendall. No word on Xavier." Finn touched on any question I might have except where Marie and David were. Did the Consociation have its own medical facilities?

"Are we waiting on the Vault then?" I could dig into

the archives while we waited for Stacey. I had plenty of new topics to research.

Finn tapped his keyboard and stood. "The Keeper's ready for us. Might as well go now."

"Keeper?"

"Keeper of the Vault." He grinned a little more cheerfully as he passed me.

"What's their name?"

"Keeper."

I followed him out the door. "Did David put you up to this? I feel like Who is on second."

Finn chuckled, stopping at the door to the weapons and ammunition lockers. Puzzled, I waited in the hall as he cleared the entrance. Maybe the Vault was just a locker. It had sounded ominous.

We crossed the room and Finn went directly for the wooden door at the back, which I'd always assumed was a closet.

"The Vault?" I asked.

"The Vault." He tapped three solid knocks, then placed his hand against the wood. We waited for a second before he tried the handle, and it opened.

Fog roiled in the closet. Even as Finn entered, it eddied around him, but didn't leak past the door frame. "C'mon. Close the door behind you. "

I stepped into the fog with my right hand held in front of me at shoulder height so I wouldn't bump into him. The air was moist and scented of sweet lilac. We should be at an outside wall adjacent to Marie's office. When the door clicked behind me the end of the hall glowed about where her couch would be on the other side of the wall. Silhouetted, Finn waited ahead, and there was enough space for me, so I stepped up beside him. "And now?"

He pointed ahead of us, and I peered at the glow. A

small silhouette, perhaps a dwarf, approached us. With each step it grew larger, as if moving with great strides from a distant tunnel. I resisted the urge to move back. "Well, this feels more ominous." My voice was a mere whisper.

The figure approached, appropriately hooded with a cowl and robe to mask their actual shape. With one last impossible stride, they stood two paces away from us. I flinched and tensed.

"Welcome, Keeper." Finn's tone was friendly, and a bit ritualistic.

"Greetings, Finn." The voice could have been Marie's, if I hadn't known better.

Finn nudged me, and I repeated his greeting. "Well — welcome, Keeper." The words were stiffly formal.

"Greetings, Kristen Winters."

I wasn't too surprised the Keeper knew my name. Why not? They had a magical portal, after all.

Finn stretched out his hand. "I have requested Yan's Pin."

The dark figure reached out with inhuman fingers which were curved instead of jointed. "I have brought Yan's Pin to your care. Return it when you are satisfied." Two of the fingers met to hold something, and then released over Finn's palm.

Finn closed his hand around something too small, or too covered in fog, for me to see. "I shall return it."

The Keeper turned, and for one moment I caught a profile of a spiked muzzle with nostrils and ridges heading up the nose. They walked away from us at the same pace as they had arrived, dwindling to some distant place.

Finn nudged me, and the pleasant scent of his dreads wafted in the air. "The Keeper. The Vault. Let's go." He turned, and I followed in misty darkness until I found the edge of the door he'd opened, then into the room where we stored our weapons.

"That was — different." I studied Finn's closed fist. "Yan's Pin?"

He opened his hand, and a silver pin no bigger than one in my grandmother's sewing room glistened against his dark palm. "Did you expect something . . ." Finn paused.

"Bigger. More ornate."

"The inscriptions are hard to read with a naked eye." He picked up the pin with his other hand and showed me the top. It looked scratched, but the closer I peered at it, the more structure it revealed.

"Aren't you afraid of losing it?" I asked.

"Oh, yeah." He grinned and dug into his jacket pocket to pull out a little purple stash box. Finn handed me the pin. "Hold it for a sec."

As I pulled the little pin from his fingers, a pulse beat through my hand similar to the sense I might get touching a door I'd warded. I saw no realm, though Finn blurred lightly for a fraction of a second. "What realm is this made with?"

He unscrewed the lid and exposed a tiny purple cloth. "Earth. The merfolk and dwarves have confirmed it." Retrieving the pin, he stuck it through the fabric and dropped it into the container.

I'd touched talismans created with the Haven realm for healing, and glimpsed the white realm for a moment. In my youth, my grandmother had promised I would grow up to have the skill to create such "charms" as she called them. My interest in the craft had waned against the allure of art, school, and boys.

Finn pocketed the box and headed for the door.

"The Keeper, a dragon-shifter?" I asked.

"Yep. Don't ask about the Vault, though. The Consociation is very protective about it. They won't let David in there anymore."

"He asked questions?"

"He shined a flashlight in the Keeper's face once. Another time, when he tried to follow the Keeper, they banned him." We exited the weapons and ammo room.

A small note had been taped to the employee area across the hall. I veered to read it.

"They've got David in there." Finn paused a few steps from our office door.

The note said, "Closed for repairs." I smiled and hoped David was healing.

"Udy wrote that." Finn grinned lightly, heading for our office.

My assumption of a Consociation medical facility vanished. I had so little understanding of the organization. Tomas's database hadn't expanded that view, but had confirmed what I did know.

"Where's Marie?" I asked.

Finn's office phone on his desk rang as we entered. He pointed toward the door in the back to her office. "Don't knock."

I couldn't tell if that was an invitation to check on her, or a caution not to disturb her. As he picked up his phone, I kept my questions to myself. With all the power the Consociation seemed to have, I expected better healing facilities than a break room and Marie's office.

"On our way, Udy." Finn put down the phone and looped back toward me. "Herta's got Wendall's autopsy report finished."

I opened the door for him. "Does it wear down a dwarf to use Earth realm magic, like it does us to use Mer or Dur-Alf?"

He raised his eyebrows and tilted his head. "Oh yeah.

She's going to be cranky. I wished Udy had just sent us an email, but she must want to speak with us."

When he opened the door to her room, this time I was prepared for the black shadow veil inside the door. As Finn passed through, I raised my hand into the darkness and followed him.

Wendall's body was not on the examining table; instead, Herta rested there as if taking a nap. Arms behind her head, she had her dwarf legs bent and one ankle crossed over the other knee. Measuring under four feet tall, her black braid appeared longer than it was, draped across the steel surface to her wide belt.

"Ah, the lumbering mountain dragged in the air-wasting frog." Her lenses floated over her purple eyes as she stared at the light above. I gathered I was the frog. At six feet in height, Finn would be exceedingly tall to her.

Udy, her lanky assistant, stood expressionless behind the table. Tablet in his left hand, he swiped across the screen with the other. His pale brown, almost orange, side-burns curled to the edge of his relaxed jaw.

Herta bounced her leg, still staring. "Earth magic. I'd assume a dwarf since we're skilled at this type of murder, though usually we would have a little more finesse. We're also tired of all you damned dimwitted witches trying to sneak into Dur-Alf. Black-eyed lumps of clay."

She gestured to the bank of steel coolers on the side wall. "Died when his C4 sliced through his spinal cord. Stopped breathing at least."

Finn nodded. "Thank you. Anything else we should know?"

Herta finally turned her gaze to us. Well, me. "Buy that cow yet?" She had a wide nose, accentuated by the floating lenses.

Unsure if she wanted an answer, I paused, then tapped

my curls, preparing to respond that I had not. I might even mention that I'd had cold pizza for breakfast.

She turned back to the ceiling. "I don't care. Get out."

Finn's face looked grim as we walked back to the office. I glanced again at the maintenance sign on the break room. In the force, when an officer was injured, you visited. I didn't know the proper protocol or tradition when dealing with vampires and dragon-shifters. Instead, I focused on the case.

"When do we leave?" I asked as Finn opened our office door.

"I need to . . ." Finn stopped speaking and I saw the reason when we stepped inside.

At the back, near Marie's office, Stacey leaned against the edge of Finn's desk watching us. A tall woman with sandy brown hair cut short to her neck, she had an athletic build. "Leave for where?" she asked.

Finn stiffened, either from the question, her presence, or that his items were askew where she leaned. "Tallahassee. I was just getting ready to see if you were in. I didn't expect you — so early."

In our office, I imagined he was about to say.

"Has there been another incident? Have they located Xavier Vasquez?" Stacey asked. Her tone told me she knew we hadn't.

"No. Pyre had intended to follow Wendall Landon's movements the morning before the attack."

"I've got your report. Pyre's not in charge. I am. Our primary focus is Xavier, and until then we have no need to find out what Mr. Landon eats for breakfast." Stacey's lips curled back into a cruel smile at her jest.

"Wouldn't you rather we be there when they find him?"

"He could be in Texas or the Carolinas by now."

"Or Tallahassee." Finn's tone had become frustrated.

"Let's hope. It's a closer flight. Work with Tomas to see if any of the merfolk's digging comes up with something." She straightened and pointed him to his chair. "Do you understand?"

Finn straightened and drew in a long breath. "Yes."

Her gaze turned to a glare, then settled on me. "The request should have come through me." She stretched her hand out to Finn, palm up.

He nodded and dug into his pocket for his purple stash box. "I should have waited until you came in."

Stacey took the box from him, tossing it lightly in the air and catching it. Glancing between us, she continued the action as she turned for Marie's office. "Herta says three days." She opened the door so we could all see inside. "I might recommend longer."

Marie, wrapped in what appeared to be a swaddling of blue velvet, floated behind her desk. Her bald head hung only a foot or so from the ceiling. Her eyes were closed, and her expression was peaceful. I saw no lifting spell from Mer that would hold her there.

"I could go to Tallahassee and check up on Marie's concerns," I said.

Finn and Stacey both turned and spoke in unison. "No."

Stacey still tossed the box as she closed Marie's office. "You must have something here to occupy your time."

I could study the archives, but that didn't seem like the right answer. "I've got cold cases to follow up on."

She tossed the box holding Yan's Pin to Finn and strode around him, eyeing the files still beside my desk. "What would you be working on?"

Over the past couple of weeks, I had been considering the massacre cold case. Van and Pyre had conducted the interviews, then the Consociation had brought in some pressure and squelched everyone. I might bring a more sympathetic tone to the victims, but the archives had consumed me. However, my attempt to shave off some of my ignorance wasn't working out. "There are two victims who have moved within an hour's drive of here, one in particular I'd like to start with."

Finn stared at his chair and let out a deep breath silently. If word came in about Xavier, we wouldn't be able to jump on the jet quickly. I'd been an idiot suggesting the interview.

"Actually, that's a bad idea. I should probably be here, in case word comes in from the APB."

Stacey studied me, then turned to Finn. "No, no. The interview on the cold case is approved. Be back by noon, if you can. Tomas will clear it for you." The same dark smile crept onto her face, and she headed for the door. "You both should check in on David first."

As the door closed behind me, I watched Finn who hadn't moved. I began to apologize for my foolishness and playing into the office politics. "I'm . . ."

He lifted a finger to silence me, pointed to the hall, then his ears. Werewolves had excellent hearing. "Let's check on David," he said.

When we exited into the corridor, Stacey was waiting at the elevator. As we crossed the hall, the elevator bell rang, but neither of us glanced back to see if she'd left.

Finn tried the employee room knob and found it locked. He tilted his head and spoke to the ceiling. "Tomas, let us in."

The speaker in the middle of the hall had a fuzz to it that made Tomas's high-pitched voice stand out. "It's secured. I'll let Dr. Southwark know you're requesting entry."

"Stacey told us to visit."

Tomas cursed and the speaker fuzzed.

A minute later, a pale man with a wart on his chin opened the door. I might not have focused on it, but he just stuck his head through. "No visitors. I can't have him talking."

I began to believe that our visit to David was a ruse from Stacey somehow. Her agreeing to let me go on an interview in the middle of a case seemed purely designed to thwart Finn somehow. Why departments became so twisted with personalities boggled me. I'd be happy when Marie was back on her feet again.

Finn started to shrug and dismiss the visit, but Dr. Southwark pursed his lips, then appeared to change his mind as he opened the door wider. "I don't want him talking."

"Are you sure?" asked Finn.

The doctor had thinning hair with a stray strand that dangled across his eyes when he nodded. "In, in."

His appearance bothered me, so I patted his arm. "Thank you so much."

The illusion haloed in the blue-green haze of the Mer realm, but held. I guessed a dwarf, because no one else would need a disguise. From the obnoxious wart, I guessed Udy had done the spell.

A hospital bed had been installed where the weights and bench had been. David rested at an incline with his eyes open and a slight smile growing on his face. An intravenous blood bag dangled off a stand, and a tube ran into his arm. An electric cooler whirred beside the bed. The air smelled of lemon sanitizer and a yeasty odor.

Besides his eyes and lips, David didn't move. Dr. South-wark scurried over to David and waggled his fingers. "Just a brief hello and well wishes. You can spend longer tomorrow."

Finn walked to the side of David's bed. "Hey. We lost the trail, but we're searching for Xavier now. Hang in there. You'll be as annoying as ever in a day or two if I know you." He snorted. "It'll please you to know Stacey's riding my ass."

David did seem to smile broader. I wasn't going to mention the case. Some men's egos made them want to crawl out of bed even with a bullet in them if they thought they were going to miss catching the perp. I could tell him that Stacey had tricked me into heading out for an interview. He might enjoy that.

"I'm new to this whole vampire healing thing. Just know I want you back with us." I glanced at Dr. Southwark. Herta had issues with vampires, but perhaps that was more personal than an overall dwarf bias.

David blinked, then rolled his eyes to check on Dr. Southwark.

I'd leave the whole interviewing a cold case debacle until tomorrow, when he might be able to enjoy it more and maybe even say something to rib at me. "We'll be back tomorrow."

"I'm going on stage," David whispered.

Dr. Southwark's eyes bulged. Udy did good work.

"Wish me luck," David finished.

Confused, I frowned, then chuckled. "Break a leg."

SEVEN

Driving out of Atlanta in what I considered Marie's Jeep, I kept shaking my head at my stupidity. Finn had been withdrawn when we'd returned to the office, but I could understand that. Stacey had made things difficult, our team members were down, and we'd lost our only solid lead, Xavier.

The trip to Newborn, Georgia took a little over forty minutes, then finding the house where Joe Capra lived took another twenty when it should have taken five. The mailbox only had numbers on one side, which appeared to be the norm. Down a dirt driveway, a subtle low house, possibly a trailer with siding, nestled in bushes in the shade.

Informed of my impending arrival, Joe waited on the porch for me. He was a young man with haunted eyes and dark circles under them. The blond stubble on his cheeks looked a couple days old. As I pulled in front of the house, he stood and shuffled down the steps to meet me. The aroma of spicy herbs and earth hung in cool air. The weather had warned of a coming cold front after some rain, but the chill seemed to have arrived already.

"Mr. Capra?" I asked, though I'd seen his picture from a happier time in his life.

"You're the agent from the FBI?" He glanced at the Jeep, then at my jacket as if looking for the holster.

I showed him my badge and he studied it as I introduced myself. "Special Agent Kristen Winters. I'm following up on the incident on New Year's Eve."

He blinked and visibly shuddered, then nodded with his head toward the house. "They said I can speak to you." Joe opened the door politely for me. "They don't want to hear no more of it. No one does."

"I do," I assured him.

There were two cushioned wicker couches inside, forming a corner. I sat where he motioned me. The screen cut the breeze, making it feel a little warmer. The scent of whiskey came from a glass where he'd been waiting. Did he drink every morning, or just when the FBI came out to dredge up the horror? I imagined the massacre had been the worst night of his twenty-two years.

"I'm going to ask about the events leading up to the time you were assaulted."

He ignored me, his hands on his knees as he spoke. His tone rose with each sentence. "I think I killed a lady. Don't know for sure. I should be in jail. Dead."

I could see the pain and fear on his face. Like my confrontation with a demon a couple weeks ago, losing control of your emotions in itself was terrifying. Hurting someone during it would be a haunting experience.

"When did you decide you were going to Jojo's? Had this been a planned outing?"

He rocked forward. "No. I was in school down in Jacksonville. Michael and I just decided that we'd go. Two days before New Year's."

"What school?" I asked to slow his nervous motion.

"UNF — University of North Florida." He gestured to the house. "My parents can't afford much more than that. Couldn't." His expression slackened. Joe had dropped out after the incident.

"What program?" I made a mental note to see if the victims were low-income.

"Criminal Justice."

I tilted my head and smiled. "Same here."

That moved him a little more toward relaxed, so I edged back to my focus. "Were you at school when you and Michael decided to go to Jojo's?" I knew they were classmates, but I dug toward something else, I just didn't know what.

"No, we were down in Five Points, hitting up some bars. Nothing major." He rocked, studying the backs of his hands. "Michael was yelling at a car and this girl runs up, hands us the cards for Jojo's. He chilled, asking if she was going to be there."

"Was she — at Jojo's?" I asked.

He frowned at my question, then slowly shook his head. "I didn't see her."

Another note for my file: check for girl handing out cards. Van's reports ran heavy with speculation and his conjectures, which aligned with everyone else's that this was a demon or jinn. However, his interview notes were not details but interpretation. He'd done the most work, and I had little to go on for the effort. Flyers had been posted for the New Year's Eve party. No one had mentioned getting an invite.

"Well, it made sense that you wanted to go, after this hot woman hands you an invite."

Joe nodded.

"What was Michael yelling about?"

"Hmm. Oh. Yeah, some guy races out of the parking lot and cuts across the sidewalk in front of us. He wasn't close to us, but Michael — he used to get hot about those kinds of things." Joe's face contorted at the last comment as emotions of concern and then pain twisted his features.

"Did you meet the DJ?" The DJ's assistant had been Van's big lead. "Toughnut was her name."

"No."

"How about her assistant?" The only name we had for the missing man was Shoo. At least we knew Toughnut's real identity.

He started to shake his head, then lifted it. "The asshole throwing beetles?"

"Yes, him." Literally, live beetles. Van hypothesized over them, but no one claimed to have been bitten or eaten one. "Did you meet him? Have any interaction with him, besides bugs?"

"No." He winced, then scowled, perhaps remembering his more brutal actions that night.

I led Joe back from the pain again by talking about school and the classes he took. Once I had him less tense, I returned to the description of the parking lot of the club when they first arrived. Other than the woman with the invitations and possible economic status, I got nothing from the interview the three prior hadn't already dug up. Everything about the rave had been normal and customary, until they all tried to kill each other.

After an hour, I thanked Joe and at least had some new questions for my next interview, which wouldn't be today. I'd fulfilled my stupidity and could return to the office and wait on Xavier or another bone-shattered corpse. Either way, I planned to be back before lunch.

I never saw a town as I left; Joe's family probably lived on the outskirts. Technically I'd grown up in the city of Ontario, Oregon. If you drove in from the west or north, my neighborhood appeared just as rural as Joe's.

EIGHT

I stepped into the office with a paper bag of deliciousness for Finn and myself. "Have you ever had chocolate croissants?"

From behind his monitor, Finn just pointed to the ceiling. "Stacey wanted you to check in when you arrived."

Whatever positive mood I'd restored with retail therapy, even better, food retail therapy, faded then shriveled to apprehension. The long drive back from the interview had worn on my patience until I vowed not to open my mouth around Stacey again. She couldn't expect a written report already. "She say why?"

He stood and eyed the bag. "Chocolate croissants? Do I have to wait?"

"One of us should enjoy the moment." I dropped my purse in my drawer and handed him the bag. "Save me one."

Finn peered inside, then inhaled. "There's only two."

"Ugh." I marched into the hall.

The floor above ours had more agents milling about. Most only gave me a cursory glance as they marched alone or in pairs. I knocked on the glazed window of Stacey's door.

The muffled bark I took as her calling me in, so I opened it and peered inside. The office had no more personalization or warmth than it had before. The bookshelf behind her was still empty, and her desk didn't even have a pen on it.

Stacey sat stiffly in her chair, head tilted down to her tablet, the sole item on her desk. She took a long, long moment before peering at me from under her eyebrows. The expression did justice to her werewolf nature. "Did you find anything?" Her tone was challenging.

I doubted the woman handing out invitations counted as a solid lead yet. "I don't think so. I have a little more to—"

She leaned back into her chair. "Pyre might coddle you, but you're the newbie. You have no idea what to even look for. Xavier is our focus. Even if that means playing solitaire at your desk." Stacey emphasized each word of her last sentence. "You wait for the call."

"You—"

"I gave you the rope." She pointed past me into the hall. "Now go swing. I expect a report in twenty in my email."

I stood there for a moment and fought the heat in my cheeks. "You are right. I was wrong to leave." I would have gotten the point without us all wasting our time and energy.

She dropped her hand. "I know. Go."

I spun on my heel as her cell rang. Carefully closing the door lightly, rather than slamming it, I heard her sharp voice call me back. "Winters."

Drawing a deep breath and expecting a more detailed reprimand, I eased the door back open to view her scowl. Her werewolf form would have likely been more inviting.

Stacey gestured with her cell phone to the side. "You're heading back to Tallahassee. Finn's screw up just cost a pregnant woman her life."

My stomach twisted. I hated when our next clue happened with someone's death.

"Yes, Ma'am." I pulled the door closed and ran for the elevator. My comms were charged and in my purse. Finn would be in the weapons room already, as I guessed we both got the news at the same time. I'd get our go bags by the printer and collect the reports. Wincing, I realized we would only need two copies.

When I entered, the printer was already whirring, spitting out pages. Our office had the sharp scent of electricity and ink. As expected, Finn was gone. He had saved both croissants, and they went gingerly into my purse. We had a lot to carry down to the Jeep.

I collated papers, glancing back at the door leading to Marie.

Finn opened the door and stopped when he found our go bags there and me collecting the last couple of pages off the printer. "How was it?" he asked.

"What?" I'd been reading about the woman, a waitress named Sally Oswald at the deli near where Wendall had died, where Xavier had been buying lunch.

"Stacey's little game. I couldn't have warned you not to leave. She would have found something worse."

I pointed to my ear where Tomas sat on the live comms.

Ammo and rifle strapped over his shoulder, Finn shrugged nonchalantly. "Tomas knows."

He grabbed his go bag, leaving me to shove reports into folders and then into my purse. Finn propped the door open as I grabbed my go bag, and we headed into the hallway.

Tomas's high-pitched voice followed us to the elevator. "Your victim, Sally Oswald, was just pronounced dead at the scene. Local FBI has allowed Investigator Dee to take the body. I have informed Stacey of the situation." He rattled off the details, though his tone didn't express the frustration Finn and I shared in a glance.

"I should have left you in Tallahassee." Finn's inflection carried self-recrimination, but we both knew that the fault was Stacey's and mine.

"That wouldn't have saved Sally." I punched the button to the elevator with a spare finger.

"No, but you might have been able to head over and intercede against Dee." He spoke sharply, and I wondered if he resented me and Stacey. "Tomas. I assume we have transport waiting to bring Sally back here."

Tomas swore. "Of course."

We stepped into an occupied elevator. A brown-haired woman moved to the back corner. Finn had the big gun case, so I let him settle inside first. She murmured to our greetings, but she wasn't an agent based on the light blouse, no holster, and no badge. We remained silent until we were out of the elevator and on our way to the back exit.

"It's not your fault," Finn said. He forced a smile. "I'm frustrated with the job, my life, Stacey, and not being able to help Pyre and David. It's leaking out. Normally I control myself better when I want everything to go my way, and as usual, they don't." He had emphasized job and life strongest suggesting that Gary's influence pressed harder than the rest.

"It's okay, Finn. It is." In him, I saw the stress which had consumed me during the time between my divorce and when I'd given up and let Jade move back with her father. After that, it'd been soft regrets and sobbing depression. I could empathize.

The stocky bearded guard who often worked the entrance opened the door at the sight of our loads. He had an easygoing expression and offered a smiling nod when I thanked him. Someday, when we weren't rushing past, I'd have to ask his name.

An hour later we were in the air and on our way to Tallahassee. Finn held up a flattened chocolate croissant, chewing thoughtfully. "Not bad."

I scraped some of the chocolate off the paper with mine. "Better when they're fluffy. I don't know why."

"Ready?" Tomas sounded annoyed.

"Video?" Finn asked then stuffed the rest of the croissant into his mouth.

Tomas swore, and his high pitch peaked even sharper. "The manager at the store refuses, says that Investigator Dee is to confirm the request."

Finn set out his folder, then pivoted toward the display I'd set up. It felt odd without Marie. "What do you have that's not in the report?"

The display brought up Sally Oswald, a selfie from the grinning face. "She was seven weeks pregnant. Just started posting about it. Her husband, Nick Oswald, is driving in from a job in Alabama. Building contractor. Neither have any arcane or craft interest or connections based on what little data I have on them. Most is through social media." The video had switched to an equally happy picture of Sally's husband and my chest hollowed.

"Twelve witnesses. Eight were customers. Three in line. Five at tables. Three coworkers and one manager. I have no confirmation without video. I'm running all the names provided. Four have popped up level one arcane interests, but nothing has risen to actual practice."

I frowned at Finn. "Level one?" I'd seen the comment in a report in the archives and hadn't followed that rabbit hole.

"Ouija, tarot, palmistry, getting a psychic reading. Even then we'll only classify with repeated interest." Finn fended off my question with his hand when I opened my mouth to interrupt. "They are matched against actual seers. If they have repeated contact with a witch of that ability, we put them right up to level two. Contact with a practitioner."

I'd definitely have to go down that rabbit hole. How many levels were there?

The screen flicked through a variety of photos, which I assumed were the customers and workers. "I've got nothing beyond this data. None of our previous witnesses cross reference, and no one from the apartments where Pyre and David were attacked."

Finn glanced at me, seeming to remember something. "Did you send Kristen the three practitioners from the apartments?"

Tomas cursed. "Of course."

"Thank you."

Guilty, I pulled out my phone. "I was driving, then Stacey, then . . ." I cut off my excuses and pulled up the team's email.

Finn grinned, if a little sadly. "Let's just see what we have. None of these incidents have anything in common. We have two with Xavier and Emily. Ignoring them for just a minute, let's look at Sally as the sole incident." He tapped the paper reports. "Again, merfolk or dwarf or Mahakala's Quartz appear our best culprits. Do we agree?"

"Yes, given how inexperienced I am. I have nothing else to offer." I hated being in the shallow end of the pool.

"Don't let that cloud your thinking. What's the questions we should be asking?"

Merfolk could change their appearance, so they could be impersonating someone. I had assumed a dwarf could create their own illusion, but Udy had obviously done Dr. Southwark's appearance. Mahakala's Quartz would require conflict.

"Tomas, was there any outburst prior to Sally's death? An irate customer?"

"None in the reports."

I pursed my lips and moved to the question about the dwarfs before annoying Tomas. "Why does Udy do Herta and Dr. Southwark's illusions? Are they incapable?"

Finn nodded. "Udy's skilled. Besides, an active persona requires energy, as it would for us. Considering how obvious they'd be if it slipped, they can't keep refreshing it while they focus on healing. A dwarf would have less difficulty, if they weren't using other magic."

"Then, like the museum visitors in Tennessee, we should circle around and make sure everyone in the deli was there. No impostors." Tugging on a curl, I watched Finn as I asked my last question. "Can merfolk change their appearance any time they want?"

Finn answered, saving me and perhaps Tomas. "No. They require reentering Earth's realm to re-skin. Is that the proper term, Tomas?"

"Close enough."

I grimaced at the tone. At least he had not lathered on the curses. "Well, without a conflict present at the first two incidents, I'd lean toward dwarf or merfolk spells using Earth, dwarves being the more likely culprits. If we're just looking at this one event."

Finn nodded slowly. "I'd agree. If we add in our situation with Xavier, we might have a renegade dwarf. One who's been masquerading for a long time."

Right after Marie and David had gone down, I'd wondered if they'd been the target. Someone could create a situation to bring them out, then hunt them. Sally's death had wiped that speculation off the board. "So, you clear up the issue with Sally's remains, and then we visit the witness list at their homes while we wait for Xavier to pop up on the radar." I wiped a smear of chocolate off my pants and unbuckled to clean it off in the bathroom. "Tomas, any option of video outside the deli, like in the street? Maybe Xavier was out there."

"None. I would have told you."

Of course he would have. I stood, wobbled a little down the aisle, and climbed into the tight stall. As soon as the water ran so I could dab at the chocolate, I needed to pee. Since I tapped the comms closed for privacy, I could hear Finn's voice talking, but not his words.

I hurried, frustrated at missing something. "What?" I asked when I stepped out.

"Dee wants to meet us at the crime scene. The deli will be closed by then, and the manager locked up for the day." Finn's tone edged on anger. "He refuses to release the body and is calling Pyre's bluff. He wants to speak to the CDC since he can't speak with Pyre."

I started to ask what Stacey could do for us, but I couldn't be sure she would. Why had she taken a position over a team which she seemed to want to fail? Maybe we didn't need the crime scene right away. We had a plan which had little to do with the deli. Sally's body needed to get out of the coroner's office. The witnesses had to be confirmed as human.

"Screw Investigator Dee. Let's coordinate with the Consociation team sent to transport the body. We can meet them at the coroner's office while Dee is waiting for us at the deli." I smiled. "Tomas, how hard would it be to interrupt his communications? Phone and radio."

"With Consociation tech, it's easy." Tomas paused. "However, I'm assuming we're not going through Stacey on this. Finn, she wants a report one hour after you land."

"Then we move quick. Bluff our way into the coroner's and get Sally out of there. We'll be on our way to interviews when Dee gets the news." I put my hands out toward Finn questioningly. How far over the line could we go?

David's voice came through the comms in a deep whisper. "Jimmy D. ain't going to like this."

"David." My voice betrayed just how happy I was to hear him.

"Your favorite bloodsucker. Aw, how sweet, you missed me."

I blushed, but didn't argue. "Are you supposed to be on the comms?"

"Are you supposed to be breaking corpses out of Jimmy D.'s jail?"

"Feeling better?" Finn asked.

"Oh, I'm fine. But how am I supposed to refuse an open bar?"

I cringed at the thought of the intravenous blood bag. He joked and still had healing to go through. Did he need a certain kind of blood if it just went directly into his veins? "Do you need a certain type?"

"I *prefer* blonde, with either sex. In women, I like athletic over just plain scrawny. The only *need* I have is willing."

I groaned dramatically and glanced at Finn. His grin appeared a little less forced. David sounded better.

"Oops." David whispered and a voice sounded in the background. He spoke louder. "I'm just checking out my vocal cords — wouldn't want to lose my singing voice." His comms cut off, and I guessed Dr. Southwark had caught him talking to us.

I had half expected to hear him rattling his mints. Chewing might be completely off the table. At least I only had to worry about Marie now, though Finn appeared to assume she'd be alright soon. The quicker we had her interfering between our work and Stacey, the better.

Finn still hadn't agreed to my plan. "What do you think?" I asked. "Get Sally's body on the road and just ignore Investigator Dee for tonight?"

Once I'd made lead detective in Grand Junction, I'd pulled maneuvers like this. My supervisors didn't like it and warned me that I wouldn't get very far, but there wasn't anywhere I wanted to go. I doubted I'd get kicked out of Pyre's Pups.

"It sounds like it's right out of Pyre's playbook. I just don't know if we should try it with Stacey on top of us." Finn chuckled. "Never mind. I'm in. What's the worst that she could do, fire me?"

CHAPTER

NINE

"Got 'em." Tomas sounded like a young gamer with that voice and his excitement. "I'm sending you coordinates now. Xavier's heading down a dead-end road. I got him on a traffic cam."

"Where?" asked Finn.

Tomas continued without answering. "Consociation servers out of Miami are popping open the video stream at a local convenience store on the corner. Thanks to them using cloud storage, no one will know."

Our monitor flashed with a few seconds of Xavier walking with a beverage down a badly paved road. Then a fast forward image of him zipping into a convenience store, and a few seconds of him leaving the parking lot. The traffic footage appeared grainy, but we had him heading back down the dirt beside the asphalt.

"Three residences on the road. Checking ownership and cross referencing. A map replaced the video. Got it. Cousin of a coworker." The image resolved to a Google satellite image and zoomed in on a house that appeared to have a few add-ons. "I've set servers to dig into their internet provider."

On the force, we would have needed a fistful of warrants, or risk our careers and evidence. I doubted the FBI was that different. The Consociation appeared to have resources more powerful than both of them. Warrants weren't an issue, especially since we weren't bringing this case to trial. We just needed to stop Xavier, if he were the one causing the deaths. Still, it creeped me out when I thought of how much Tomas knew of practitioners. We were probably watched with as much abandon.

Tomas swore a short stream. "I'm pretty sure Xavier wasn't in town during Sally's death. I've got a half-hour call to his mother through that time and at this location. I've got her calls tracked, but she talks to a lot of people all over Tallahassee. I had asked Stacey if I could tap Xavier's family phones, just for voice recognition. She said no."

"Well, if Xavier didn't kill Sally, and Emily wasn't in the deli, we're back to dwarf."

"I'm going to keep facial recognition tracking him, whatever your call is."

"Agreed," said Finn.

"Sally's body first. Then we clear up Xavier? Then interviews?"

Finn tapped his armrest. "Once we get Sally released, *we* aren't going after Xavier or doing interviews. You'll need to stay a good bit away, on comms. I'll be going in with Yan's Pin."

I leaned forward to complain, but his firm expression stopped me. He motioned to my seatbelt, and I scrambled as the jet's engine throttled. We were near time to land. I'd be backup in this investigation — at best. He'd likely drop me at the hotel.

When we exited the tiny airport, the local FBI handed

off keys to a sedan with two vests in the trunk. Finn didn't even bother trying to get an answer for their weak support in this case; we both knew Stacey hadn't put in much effort. Maybe if she could let us all fail, she'd start a new team more under her control. My little plan with the coroner's office might expedite that.

The fake pine air freshener stunk like a porta-potty. I pulled up Tomas's coordinates for where Sally's body was being held as we wove through the city streets. Where some cities were planned as grids and squares, much of Tallahassee had been built around sweeping curves. The closer we got, the more I second-guessed my none too brilliant plan.

We pulled around the side of the two-story Department of Health building, and Tomas identified the emergency transport vehicle belonging to the Consociation. I didn't see anything out of the ordinary. The two people who stepped out were black women close to my age.

Finn hopped out with a cordial smile. "Hey, I'm Finn, this is Kristen. We're still having problems getting official avenues to open up, but we'd really like to get this body out of there."

One of the women stepped forward. "I'm Nicole, but I'm not about to jump into anything sketchy. That's y'all's game." She had a deep southern accent, and her partner nodded warily in agreement.

I'd assumed, since they worked with the Consociation, that they'd be as cavalier as Marie. Finn glanced back then shrugged. "Wait here. We'll see what we can do."

Feeling less confident than Finn appeared, I strode with him to the front of the building. "Do you think this is going to work?" I asked.

"Unlikely," Tomas answered.

Finn grinned and kept walking.

Like most government buildings, the entry was spacious and filled with slogans attesting to their dedication to service. The office had a clean, disinfected odor and a receptionist who gave an annoyed expression when she spotted us.

Finn leaned on the corner, his badge palmed. "How are you doing?"

"Fine. What can I help you with?" Her tone easily said to please leave.

Finn adjusted to a quicker, all business tone. "Afternoon, Agent Billings to pick up a body. Sally Oswald. Who do we talk to?" He peered down the closest hall.

"Amanda Prescott. Is she expecting you?"

"Not me specifically, but . . ."

"Have a seat. I'll call her out here." The receptionist picked up a phone and punched buttons.

"We can just head to her office . . ."

The receptionist pointed to the chairs. We could hear her talking quietly as we walked to the seats.

"This is not working out the way I planned," I whispered.

"Give it time." Finn sat with his long legs kicked out and crossed, though he didn't appear relaxed. "She's just doing her job. The one we need to work on is this Amanda Prescott." His eyes darted from the hall to the two secured doors, ignoring the bathrooms and water cooler.

Outside of government agencies, badges worked fairly well at opening doors. Most people assumed that they had few rights to refuse, and law enforcement perpetuated that belief. Within the machine, you knew it was all rules and forms. When the right person spoke with your boss, rules changed. That was where Stacey was supposed to come in.

Amanda Prescott scurried out fifteen minutes later with blue-rimmed glasses low on the bridge of her nose and sharp brown eyes focused on us. She had a few pounds on me and wore a long flower-printed dress which my grandmother would have called a frock. "Special Agent Billings?"

Finn smoothly slid up to greet her. "Yes. Amanda Prescott?"

"I don't have the proper paperwork to release Ms. Oswald's body."

"According to Investigator Dee? He has his own agenda. It might not be in your best interest to get in the way of a Federal investigation, because of his — personal reasons." Finn tilted his head. "Have you discussed this with your supervisor?"

Tomas's droll comment sounded as if he'd been easily prepared. "Charles Upshaw."

"Charles Upshaw?" Finn finished, giving her an opportunity to respond.

The edges of her lips curled as if she might break a smile, but she didn't. "Mr. Upshaw has reviewed the situation, and concurs."

"It's the mayor after that." Tomas piped in.

"If you have that on record, then I'll have the orders directed to him. Would you be able to provide me the correspondence, or are you relating a personal conversation?" Finn's tone had firmed. A flicker of uncertainty flashed across her face and Finn's voice softened. "I would be comfortable with this landing on his desk, if I knew it was documented."

"He's not available. There's a dinner he'll be attending . . ."

"Where?" asked Finn in a delightfully casual manner. "We'll head there now."

"Tomorrow, he'll be . . ."

Finn shook his head. "Thirteen hours and we'll be

working with the CDC under emergency orders." He played Marie's hand, and I had to turn as the woman's expression grew shocked.

We were close. Lower-level administration often balked at simple requests, but once they turned complicated, they had to balance their own career if a situation turned messy. I held back a smile.

Banging open, the door swung too far as Investigator Dee stormed through. "I thought you might try some BS." He nodded to the receptionist. "Seems like the way you all roll." His study of Amanda appeared a little less familiar, and possibly hostile. His close-cropped hair seemed to bristle as he approached us. "You will explain — to me —what is happening. I've got citizens dropping and some commotion being covered up that involved your boss."

Finn turned slowly to face the officer. "The FBI does not report to you. We all have a chain of command to follow. You have your orders."

Investigator Dee smiled. "That's what you don't get. My commander, Major Osborne, is digging into the FBI's request, and so far no one is even bothering to respond. Especially to your allegations that the CDC is involved. Nothing happens until he gets answers." He leaned in and punched a finger toward Finn's chest, stopping short by an inch. He spoke each syllable with a punctuated emphasis. "You don't get the body."

My pulse rose as he seemed intense enough that he might resort to pushing, and I didn't know how Finn would react. I couldn't use magic or my weapon.

Standing calmly in the face of the tirade, Finn spoke quietly. "You and your commander are making a mistake."

Amanda stepped forward. "Dammit Dee, you said you didn't have the proper paperwork, nothing about refusing the request. I don't like being lied to just to further your career or whatever agenda you have now."

Investigator Dee waved off Amanda's comment, nearly hitting her. "Shut up, Amanda. Go back to your little office."

"Shut up?" She appeared about to clock the officer, and I'd be willing to risk a small binding to pin him down.

We all paused when Sally's husband, Nick, burst through the door with tears streaming down his face. "Where is she? God, they . . ." As tall as Finn, he had a worker's build and focused on the officer's uniform immediately. He stomped toward Investigator Dee as if he intended to pry the information out of him. "What happened? They won't tell me anything." As he reached forward, Dee stepped back, left hand out and right resting on his holster.

Marie, sounding tired, spoke through the comms. "Take a step back, both of you."

Even as she spoke, I sensed a calming wave roll over me. Finn moved quickly, and I followed. Nick's eyes lost focus.

The door opened gently, and a short woman stepped inside. She wore a lavender blouse and skirt which flowed to her ankles. Older than me, she had a kindly face and stopped two paces inside the building. Her presence was the source of my calm, and her effect on the investigator and Nick became obvious as they sagged.

"Move Amanda Prescott away from the others. Both of you," Marie spoke quietly, but I was eager to comply.

Finn and I circled over to the woman, and I touched her arm. "Come with us."

She nodded, and a timid smile touched her lips. "Okay." She let me guide her by her hand toward the hall from where she'd appeared.

Investigator Dee turned with a confused and glazed expression. "Hold on." He seemed strained to say even that much.

Finn flashed one of his broad smiles to the officer. "Wait here." I almost reacted to the command, but we moved farther away from the strange woman at the door.

Her eyes squinted from thick folds under her eyes, and the wrinkles added to her kind disposition. She had to be from the Consociation. Her body motionless, she held her hands in front of her and watched us depart.

"You had the right plan, just not the resources to complete it." Marie spoke haltingly, as if with effort.

"The husband should be able to see his wife," I said to Marie, "to say goodbye."

Amanda heard me, and thinking I spoke to her, slowed. "Yes."

Finn placed his hand lightly on her shoulder and encouraged her forward.

"Don't reply to me. That husband does not need to remember his wife in the state she's in. He'll be troubled, but when we return the body, she will be put into better shape."

The scent of disinfectant grew sharper, and the eerie silence left only our footsteps echoing off the walls. Amanda blinked as we walked a few steps and then she withdrew her hand from mine.

"Tell her to check her emails; the request has been sent directly to her. Her supervisor is copied on the form."

"Let's go to your office." I smiled, the fog lifting from my own mind. "You should have everything you need in your email."

"That's not normal procedure." Her earlier stubbornness returned.

"Nothing about this is normal." I laughed, trying to

relax her again. "If the Tallahassee police department isn't going to follow procedure, then we'll have to work this out with you. The papers are in order, you'll see."

"They don't have the authorization to refuse the request, certainly not at their level." Amanda nodded to herself, pleased at her rationalization. She'd work against Dee by helping us.

"Thank you," I said.

Five minutes later we left Amanda sitting quietly at her desk. Even at this distance in the back of the building, I could sense a soothing presence.

Nicole and her cohort entered through the side door. The rattling wheels of the gurney gnawed at my artificial calm. I half expected Dee to escape the Consociation woman, but no one interfered.

The gray-walled room smelled sickly and foul despite the antiseptic disinfectant. Ventilated sinks lined one wall with coils of transparent hoses. The center table had power outlets for the coroner's equipment, and I was grateful Sally wasn't on it. They brought her out of the cold steel wall, sealed in a black body bag.

When they identified the corpse, Sally's skin was a blackened purple, and I had to turn away. Her young face appeared slack, and the only color which appeared normal was her light brown hair and the whites of her eyes. Intense lights etched my momentary glimpse into my memory. Nick did not need to see his wife like this.

We would have failed to get the body without Marie and the Consociation's help. She'd said my plan was correct, but it lacked any proper forethought. My default bluster wouldn't work in dealing with local governments. I had already placed myself outside the very departments I had been working for, starting with the werewolf I'd killed a couple months ago.

After we escorted the body out to the Consociation vehicle, Marie spoke. "Report."

Nicole moved quickly to stow Sally's body, so we left them. No one had come bursting out of the building behind us. Amanda would deal with the worst of Dee's ire. What would they remember of the Consociation interference?

"Tomas found Xavier, Pyre." Finn led us to the car. "We're headed there now, but he is likely not our perpetrator."

"Interview and confirm. Take precautions." Her words were coming out slower and more deliberate.

"I'll leave Kristen in the car and approach him. I have Yan's Pin." Finn started up the car.

I bristled, but didn't argue. My ego still stung from my badly executed idea to retrieve the body. It might be best if I got a little more experience before barging forward.

"You're proficient with the rifle, Kristen." Marie made it a statement, likely knowing more about my past than I wanted her to. "Keep hidden, but have Finn in sight as much as you can." It pained me to hear her difficulty even speaking.

"Will do."

We drove out to the main road; a police department's truck was parked at the front doors with its lights flashing. Dee had been in such a hurry to stop us, he hadn't turned them off.

"Who was the woman?" I asked. I could have asked what she was. No witch I knew could cause such an effect. Rumors about the Salmhalla realm spoke of compulsion.

"Old lady with squinty eyes?" asked David over the comms.

"David," Marie warned.

"Pyre's daughter," he answered.

Finn frowned and glanced at me. Perhaps our help had not come from the Consociation, but Marie directly. I put aside any questions for later, when I wouldn't have my comms on. Pointing to the left, I navigated Finn to the coordinates Tomas had sent for Xavier's location.

"How do you think this is going to go?" I asked Finn, pointing left at the next intersection.

"If Xavier is innocent, I'll explain I need to conduct a simple interview and then leave him to his life." Finn sighed.

He would know if Xavier wasn't innocent if the man, or something else, tried to attack him in the same fashion that had Marie and David convalescing. Except, if Yan's Pin didn't work, he'd end up like Sally.

"Try to draw him outside, where I have a shot." I hated the idea of killing a man — anyone.

"Plan on it." Finn exhaled, blowing and almost whistling. Did he think of Gary at this moment? I'd be thinking of Jade.

"Aim for the royal jewels," said David.

I frowned, searching for the joke. "What? Why?"

"Head shot for a dwarf." David wasn't joking. "Debilitating for a man, take my word for it."

TEN

"Tomas, yards to door from our location?" Finn crouched by the back door of our borrowed vehicle, putting on his Kevlar vest. I cringed as he slipped it over his chest. He'd pierced Yan's Pin through his skin, on the left side.

"Two-twenty-four."

"Aim for the pelvis," Finn told me.

We'd pulled to the side of the dead-end road where the brush led into a forest just showing new green growth. I'd moved to the driver's seat, and we'd left the engine running. With the passenger window rolled down, I rested the muzzle on the frame as I attached the scope.

The pale green, one-story house where Xavier holed up had a white truck pulled under a pole barn to the right side. Low hanging branches from a live oak obscured the front of the vehicle and the entire side. I had a clear view of the porch, front windows, and wooden door. A row of cone-shaped evergreens lined the road, cropping the left corner of the porch. A shaggy lawn stretched along the sides of the old wood building. My pulse raced. The sun hung mid-afternoon in the sky; an hour later it would have interfered with my vision.

I'd gotten used to the fake pine scent, and then I bumped into it as I tested my sight. My grandmother would have told me to always fire a weapon before you needed it, and she wouldn't have used a scope.

"Those 6.5 rounds will hit before the second is over. If I look like I'm in trouble, take two shots and then aim for the head."

"I don't tend to be trigger happy, but I don't like this situation. If you fall, then it might be too late." I checked my chamber for the third time.

"We don't know for sure." Finn strapped on his holster and rolled his shoulders. "I'm hoping Xavier was coincidence, and he's just being careful staying out of our sights. I'll do a quick interview, then let him know it's safe to go back to work. If we need to dig deeper later, we'll know where he is." He slid on his jacket and tugged into it. "I'm hoping we'll be on our way in fifteen minutes. Glad it's not a warm day."

From my seat, the farthest structure down the road was a two-story brown house with an already green lawn and three kids running in circles with a dog. They were far enough away not to be a concern, but not optimal if had to shoot at a running target heading toward them. Nearly at the end on my side of the street would likely be a house tucked deeper in the woods; I could only see a red mailbox.

I focused my breathing and checked the sight again. I could see the stain in the ratty blue lawn chair in the shade. I had one pale support from the porch blocking the right edge of the front door, but it shouldn't be a problem.

Finn stood up. "I'm heading in, Pyre."

"We're blind. Tomas has nothing to work with. Talk often. Kristen, don't forget to narrate what you see."

"Break a leg," said David. The joke was getting old.

Striding quickly across the pitted asphalt, Finn made his way for the driveway. As his jacket flapped, he held it closed. I settled into my awkward position and watched the two windows and door through my scope.

The front entrance had a beveled decorative window to let in light, but it was too high up and warped to give me any view inside. In every window, white-backed curtains hung without a seam exposed. The eaves and the porch roof shaded the entire front. Knowing I was tense, I sang the poppet song to myself, mentally to avoid David's quips. Finn had turned off the drive and strode across the grass toward the stairs of the porch.

"He's on the porch," I said as Finn climbed the steps.

Through our comms, we could hear his three crisp knocks on the door. "FBI, Agent Billings." Finn stepped back. "We just want a quiet conversation with Xavier Vasquez."

The curtain moved, and I centered in an older, brown-skinned woman peering out with wide eyes. Her lips moved as she spoke to someone else. "Woman in window, watching Finn."

He stepped back, taking one of the stairs down. His eyes flicked to my right where the truck was parked. I pulled off the scope and found nothing, but couldn't see past the tree.

"Someone exited a side door. North side." Finn remained half on the step and raised his voice. "We just want to talk."

"I've got nothing with this tree in my way." I glanced to the far side, searching for a runner. No one moved through the brush covered field, cleared long ago of trees and left to grow wild.

When Finn reached for his holster, he spoke sharply. "Gun. It's Xavier going for the truck."

I kept off the scope, searching for a sign of Xavier or anyone. A gunshot cracked and a motion flickered near Finn. He didn't fire, but crouched at the railing, weapon trained on the truck. Everything in me screamed to jump out of the car and run to where we could pin Xavier down. I should have put on my Kevlar vest. Either Xavier didn't have the ability to shatter Finn's bones, or Yan's Pin worked. "I don't have him from here. I'm coming out."

"Stay put," Marie said.

My pulse raced and blood flushed up my neck. "Understood."

Xavier fired again, and Finn returned a shot. I searched the area and found the kids gone. No one moved on our street.

At the left corner, the porch wrapped around the side. Between the conical trees and the house, I had a slim view. There, a shape moved, creeping up behind Finn. "Behind you. Porch."

Finn skittered down the steps, adept at remaining a small target for being so tall. He shrunk behind the steps and porch.

I twitched, but had been ordered to stand down. Anger flashed at Xavier and whoever was closing in on Finn. If he had just listened instead of reacting, no one needed to be hurt.

Xavier fired, ripping off shreds of the railing.

"Clear my six." Finn spoke low and firm, counting on me.

In the scope a young man, a boy of fourteen or fifteen, crouched with a gun. My chest hollowed, filling with ice. Any anger at him or Xavier withered at the sight of him. I could likely make the shot and kill him. In his position, he'd be little more than body mass and shins. I couldn't let him take another step, or they'd have Finn pinned.

This terror, killing a child, had haunted me since the academy. They trained you for it and if you had a clear weapon in this kind of circumstance, you took the shot. I'd never been confronted with it until today.

The boy raised his foot to take another step, and I snapped through the crusty Dur-Alf realm. I hadn't even realized my finger had come off the trigger. The binding spell flew, obscured by the distance. If I missed, I would have just risked Finn's life; if it worked, I'd saved the boy.

He stiffened when my binding spell wound around him. His muzzle flashed and a bullet tore into the porch, a yard from Finn's back.

"I got him. Bound." I paused, barely a second, waiting for recrimination. No one spoke on comms, but Xavier took a shot again. "I'm exiting. Staying on this side of the road. I'm going to try and bind Xavier if I can see him."

"Far side of the truck," Finn said. "You should have a clear sight of him easily."

Marie didn't stop me.

I brought the rifle with me in my left hand, digging fingers into Dur-Alf with my right. My earlier anger and resentment grew again. Xavier had foolishly decided to have a shootout with the FBI. He'd dragged a young boy in with him. Maybe he had something going on besides Mahakala's Quartz.

Running across the street would have given me a better view, but I had already risked Marie's anger. Would she have shot the boy? I felt my tether to his bind still draining my energy, but the speed at which my heart raced, it wasn't a problem.

To the side of a clump of dripping sphagnum moss and a branch of tiny gray-green leaves, I found Xavier. He was firing from behind the engine block, popping up to take a shot, partially obscured from Finn by the windshield, then dropping back down. His body tilted toward the front grill, positioning for another shot when I sent my binding spell, aiming for his legs. A good bind didn't matter if you caught torso or legs; once it wound around a portion of the body, the person was immobilized.

Xavier hit the ground like a rock, both arms pinned to his right leg. "Xavier clear," I called through the comms. My pulse still raced, but my anger diminished with a deep breath.

"Hold position," said Finn. The tree blocked my view of him until he came around the corner.

I saw the woman look out a side window, her face strained in fear. "Woman in window. No weapon."

Finn came around the back of the truck, grabbed Xavier's feet, and dragged him out of sight from the front of the house. "Watch my six. Keep your distance."

The large tree's leaf-heavy branches didn't make it easy, but I found a position to watch the side of the house and the back of the truck. Finn dug through Xavier's pockets and pulled open his shirt. I assumed he searched for the crystal.

"Nothing in his pockets. No jewelry except for a silver cross. Clear. Release Xavier's binding."

Marie finally spoke; the first time since her one admonishment for me to stay clear. "We're going to have to bring in the two you bound. We've got cause, but it complicates matters."

"Slightly." Tomas cursed. "I've got Tallahassee police department responding. I didn't intercept in time. Local FBI is on their way. Consociation detainment is forty minutes out."

I flourished my hands in the air, as if Marie could see

me. "Would you rather I had killed them? The boy is a teen."

"Go help Finn." Marie sighed audibly without answering me.

The older woman disappeared from the window as I jogged into view. Finn knelt on Xavier's back cuffing his hands. The man cried in Spanish, near hysterically.

"I'm going for the boy, before she reaches him and the gun." I no more wanted to shoot her than her son or whatever relation he might be to her.

Racing for the porch stairs, I heard her shriek. I could imagine that my magic might make him seem dead. Finn had Xavier up and nodded as I passed behind the truck. Rifle held pointing down on my left side, I dragged another binding from Dur-Alf in case the gun wasn't firmly in the boy's grip, and she'd decided on vengeance.

I found her folded on the wooden slats of the porch, sobbing face to face with the child. His rigid grip locked around the gun, a small, stupid 22. He lay twisted on his side. Grabbing the weapon from his unresisting fingers, I couldn't just let her believe he was dead. I released my bindings and let the boy jerk back into motion.

He didn't run. Sobbing as hard as the woman, the boy grabbed onto her. She gasped and continued to cry, but with elation and relief. I didn't care if they ran. He'd been emotional, and would pay for it according to Marie. My pulse started to slow. The air had a sour tinge of vinegar to it, possibly from our team's ammo.

We were no closer to the culprit than we had been minutes ago, but now Xavier and the boy would be in trouble. I had a part in that, using my magic. With an expression as frustrated as mine, Finn walked toward me, pushing Xavier. Our suspect's eyes bulged and his nostrils flared as he peered at us in horror. I pocketed the wayward boy's weapon in my jacket.

From my back pocket, I pulled a plastic cuff tie and stared at the woman and boy. "I'm clear here. Cuffing the boy." I took a step forward, and smelled his urine. "Ma'am, I need to cuff him now."

Neither stopped crying nor responded in any way that indicated they heard me. Finn walked Xavier up the steps and watched the windows and doors of the house. We might have more residents.

Careful to keep some distance, I clasped the boy's right wrist where he held the woman's shoulder. They both reacted as he yanked, trying to free his hand. Her eyes glared, damp and wide. She trembled as she touched his forearm, as if she might help him. Her face slackened with resignation, and she pulled her hands to her chest, speaking to him in Spanish.

As his muscles relaxed, I pulled his arm back and cuffed one wrist, then the next. I left him with his mother. "Secure."

Finn had Xavier kneeling and facing the wall beside the door. "Is there anyone else inside?"

Xavier shook his head.

Tomas cursed in the comms. "Inspector Dee has ordered his people to cordon off the end of the street and wait for him to arrive."

"Local FBI?" Finn asked.

"Ten minutes out. You should be able to see the end of the street from your position."

Under the pole barn, the white truck had bullet holes in the front panel. Beyond that the empty lot stretched to the back of a dingy white convenience store. A large oak obscured part of the intersection, but we could make out the back of a squad car with its flickering lights.

We had ten minutes before we received reinforcements and a half hour before we could remove our detainees. We'd have to search the house properly. Xavier might have left the crystal inside, but I doubted it. A dwarf was my present contention, though that theory still had holes.

"Finn, intercept Investigator Dee. I'm working on his supervisor. Call in the Kuru; I don't want any of our rounds left on the property." Marie's tone was healthier, more robust than earlier. "Kristen, stay with Xavier and watch the house."

I watched Finn jog toward the road and then lean against a porch post in view of the intersection. A second police vehicle arrived, pulling around the first and disappearing behind the tree.

"Xavier, we are going to be here a while. Turn around and sit against the house, legs out. I feel my knees bruising just watching you."

He turned his head, peered at me, then nodded. Arms cuffed behind his back, the maneuver took a minute. "Who is the young boy?" I asked.

"Ricky."

"Is the woman his mother?"

"Elaina."

The tree blocked any view of Finn I might have, and our comms were live. I straightened and approached the mother and son. "Bring Ricky over here. Have him sit against the house."

"What will happen to him?" Elaina asked.

"He pulled a gun on a Federal officer. It's not up to me."

Her hands trembled as she prompted her boy. Even as she stood with him, she sagged and her shoulders hunched.

"He's a minor." I meant it as a comfort, but neither of

them reacted; they just shifted to a spot a few feet from Xavier and sat.

Investigator Dee swore at Finn. I could tell by the tone and cadence before he was close enough for the comms to pick up detail. "I don't know what the hell you have going on here, but you'll have some answers for me."

Finn's voice was smooth, unruffled. "Ask away."

Dee paused, but when he spoke, his voice came through sharply, as if he stood right in front of Finn. "Who are you?"

"That's an easy one. Special Agent Finn Billings."

"You know what the hell I meant. Who are you people? Where are you from?"

"Our team is based out of Atlanta. I'm sure you know that already. When you say who are we, do you mean what department are we in?"

"What is the Department of Risk Containment?"

"We are a small team; you've met most of us, who deal with exactly what it sounds like. If there's a risk outside of someone else's scope, we're set to go deal with it."

"And what — exactly — are you dealing with here in Tallahassee? What the hell is going on?"

"That is a question for your supervisor to push upstairs. I can't answer that."

"You will." Dee's voice came through loudly, as if he'd gotten closer.

Finn remained silent, and I imagined the investigator's fuming glare. In Grand Junction, we'd had a couple cases where we cooperated with the FBI and one with the NSA. None were forthcoming with information. It was frustrating, but you didn't rise to Dee's level without dealing with it. "He's new in his position, I'd bet." I said.

"Three months since he joined the Tallahassee police

department's Violent Crime Unit." Tomas rattled off the information in his high pitch.

"His major is a frustrating man," said Pyre. "I've almost got the next in command, but they're trying to circle back to Stacey, who's unavailable." Her last comment didn't disguise her disapproval.

Dee's voice became less agitated, and he'd moved back from Finn's comms as he spoke. "Nobody is getting in or out until I give them the all clear. Active shooters."

Marie's voice rose over our comms. "I'm done playing. David, you up to it?"

David's voice deepened. "Yep."

I blinked when Stacey's gruff voice continued after a moment's pause. David's voice sounded a perfect a match for Stacey's. "Soft tissue. Nothing for the doc here to get freaked out about. Besides, I'm just about ready to be up and about. Give me twelve hours, and I'll be ready for Tallahassee." As quickly, he chuckled and continued in his own voice. "I'll blister his ear and leave him spinning. What's a good Florida senator's name to throw around?"

"Tomas, connect David to the number I was just on." She sighed. "Keep it short, but get Dee replaced. This is the second order they stymied." Marie paused, sighing. "I'll probably end up with the major. Whoever they pick, have them call me."

By the time the local FBI arrived, Investigator Dee was repeating, "Yes, Sir," as he retreated from Finn.

Xavier had begun murmuring comments in Spanish to both the boy and mother, apologies from the sounds of it. My stomach growled when an errant breeze brought the scent of barbecue wafting past us. I glanced at the car with my go bag and snacks, then back at the huddled group on the porch. Guilt twitched at my lips, but I couldn't offer any comfort.

An hour later, two women in dark suits escorted Ricky and Xavier into a tinted SUV. The husband, a coworker of Xavier, stood on the roadside holding his crying wife. All of it could have been avoided. I disliked dealing with the family, the soft victims in law enforcement.

Finn had cleared the house, and an abundance of caution had kept me and the four local agents from entering. As the Consociation took their son, the couple had to remain off their property under the watchful eyes of Federal agents.

"David will not be joining you tomorrow," Marie said over the comms.

"No tears," jibed David.

"Finn, what's your timeline for moving on to interviewing the customers and staff at the diner?"

"I'll be done here in half an hour, Pyre."

"Feed Kristen, and then work with Tomas to track them down."

I blushed at Pyre's comment. Eating regular meals kept me from adding curves I didn't want.

ELEVEN

Our first interview was with a deli patron who'd been at the end of the line when Sally collapsed and died. We sat in the witness' incense-drenched apartment just three blocks from the restaurant. Her living room centered around her television with a cornered, black couch occupying most of the space.

In her forties, Margaret Worth had fading brown hair and a dour face. We heard about her physical ailments more than the scene at the deli.

"I'm lactose intolerant, so the deli is the only place for me to have a fresh sandwich."

"I'm sure," Finn said. I wasn't. "So you're in line . . ."

"Just like any other day. Except of course for poor Sally. I saw in the news she was pregnant. I had no idea. My sister was the same way, barely showed until the end. I wouldn't have been able to carry a full term — I'm pre-diabetic. I can't eat anything sweet at all."

"That has to be difficult. So before Sally collapsed, did you happen to look outside at all? Anyone stand out? We're trying to find more witnesses."

"What's to witness? She just fell to the floor. Made an awful noise and had the whole staff screaming." Margaret adjusted her blouse, glancing at the television. She likely had a show she wanted to watch.

"We'll be done soon," I promised. "So far, we haven't learned much about what might have caused Sally's collapse. We're looking for people who might have seen something odd."

"Nothing odd. People taking forever to place a simple order. Someone's card got declined."

"Well, were they upset, about their card?" I asked.

"Not at all. Sally ran it a couple times for the lady, but that was it. Happens to people all the time. They don't plan ahead." Margaret glanced at the remote on the cushion beside her. "I always plan to spend a good ten minutes in line."

Finn straightened. "So, no one outside who you remember?"

Margaret frowned and shook her head. "I'm looking at who's ordering and how long they'll take."

Finn stood, and relief washed over the woman's face. She touched the remote, but left it on the couch. "Thank you for your time," he said gracefully.

As we left, I spoke quietly. "I got nothing from her except impatience to watch her shows." We still had an hour or so of daylight left.

"Agreed. Tomas, do we have access to video yet?"

Tomas snorted. "Useless. Overhead of the cash register, and a second camera at the back door."

Finn raised his eyebrows and shrugged. "Too much to hope for, I guess."

We climbed into the car, and he seemed to sag. I grabbed my water and peered at him as I drank. Finn nodded to my phone and I pulled up our next stop. "Well, she was human."

"Seemed so."

Pyre spoke over the comms. "Hold up. Tomas has something suspicious, and I'm digging into it."

My nerves were still rattled from the shooting with Xavier, so I took a deep breath, nervous at what might be changing. We planned on interviews until nine p.m., then getting hotel rooms. There were more names on the list than we could handle in one night, especially if they dragged on as much as the last one had.

"Get back over to the coroner. We have another body from one o'clock today, just after Sally." Pyre sounded healthier, and a bit miffed.

I pulled up the map on my phone as Finn put the car into reverse. "Is this something Dee kept from us?" he asked.

"Car accident. On-duty tech didn't catch the similar signs on intake." Pyre coughed. "Skip the coroner's. Tomas, send someone to the coroner's directly; we shouldn't have a problem any longer. Send Finn and Kristen the location of the incident and traffic report."

"We'll check out the scene," Finn said. "Maybe you'll have leads for us from traffic cams."

I pulled up the new location and mapped us, directing Finn out of the parking lot. We had gained too many leads for the two of us to cover. The names of the victims blended with those we interviewed, and still I couldn't pin down whether we were after a dwarf in disguise or someone with a magical artifact. The tension knotted in my chest, and I took deeper breaths as I dug into my reports, emailed from Tomas.

"George Dillon. Park Avenue, again. At Meridian Street, just a couple blocks from the deli and the intersection where the first victim died." The timing was only four minutes between Sally and George. I zoomed out to search for apartments. "Tomas, can you sort the witnesses by the proximity of their residences to the first death?"

"Of course. You only have one witness to add for the latest death, a woman walking north on Meridian."

"One?" I asked out of surprise, not meaning to question Tomas's information.

Still, he swore. "Yes, one."

I pulled up the report, motioned Finn to take the next left, and read aloud for his sake. "2010 red Hyundai Genesis traveling eastbound on East Park Avenue veers to the right intersecting sidewalk at southeast corner, crosses lawn, and crashes into steps of house at 501 East Park Avenue. Loud music blaring from vehicle. Witness reports no other vehicles involved and no other pedestrians. Tenants of 501 exit, two pedestrians cross to north side-walk, and multiple cars slow on East Park Avenue but don't stop. Witness and tenants attempt to aid driver who is uncommunicative and possibly dead on impact." I skimmed the rest. "The difficulty the EMTs had removing the body sounds like our case. I don't have the witness statement."

"Not available yet," Tomas replied. "I've got your witness sorting done, both in list form and plotted on an area map of Tallahassee. Two deli customers were not locals and appear only at the end of the list."

"Thank you, Tomas." I cringed when I realized how infrequently I had ever said that. He supplied us with a ton of information and quicker than anyone I'd ever worked with, and I took it for granted. I'd change that.

Finn pulled us into a parking lot across the street. The driver had mowed down a stop sign and bent the pedes-trian crossing sign, dug up sections of the lawn, and flattened the hedges near the porch of the two-story brick residence. A blonde woman spoke with a man dressed in green overalls; she gestured at the damage.

Finn stepped out. "No skid marks. Didn't even try to stop."

I grimaced, imagining driving as bones broke inside. He wouldn't have been able to brake or turn the steering wheel to avoid the impact that would crush his organs. I hoped that like Wendall, our first victim, his spine had snapped before he could experience pain. "Well, the stop sign would have slowed it, and the grass is scraped off where the lawn rises at the front of the building. Is a Hyundai Genesis low?"

"Appears so." Finn walked us across the street.

The hedges were folded into what would have been brick stairs, but they were broken into a pile of rubble. The woman noted us striding toward the scene and paused her conversation. I could smell gas and oil wafting from the lawn.

"Can I help you?" she asked. She was a thin woman with dyed blonde hair, with crow's feet around her eyes and wrinkles around her mouth. The worker she had been talking with studied the yard. His overalls were stained with sweat and dirt; I guessed he was here to take care of her landscaping.

Finn showed his badge. "Special Agents Billings and Winters. We're here to look at the accident scene." He offered his hand. "Are you the owner?"

Her lips tightened as if annoyed, but she gave him a cursory shake. "Yes."

"Where you here when it happened?" Finn hadn't reacted to her handshake and gestured to the house.

"I was cleaning." She continued when he waited. "Upstairs."

Finn nodded toward the windows. "Did you look out the windows from there?"

She sighed. "Immediately. I heard the crash, then his music through the closed window." Her exasperated tone softened. "I saw the back of the car and the damage from there. I ran downstairs, but I couldn't have been able to save him." The woman shuddered and I remembered Marie's pallor, and she wasn't even human.

"When you looked out the window, did you see another car, or anyone walking, crossing the road?" Finn motioned to the street, partially turning to point.

"No, I . . ." She tilted her head. "There was a woman cutting diagonally across. They do that. It's dangerous. The speeding here is atrocious."

I turned. The parks formed a median that ended at this intersection, and on the next block, the sidewalk resumed across from the scene of the accident. Someone walking in this direction from the deli might cross here.

"Can you describe her?" Finn asked.

"Yes, please," said David. I'd forgotten he was on the comms.

"No. I was looking at my yard. Worried about the driver." Her tone grew sharper. "Light brown hair, I guess. Black T-shirt. Leggings."

"Bah," commented David with intended humor. I tried not to smile, hoping he was getting better. He had said he could control the pain.

I checked traffic, then walked the crosswalk in the direction from where the driver, George, would have been coming. The deli was only a few blocks down Park Avenue at the intersection where the first death occurred. These deaths were caused by someone local, possibly quite oblivious to their magic. The crystal seemed the most likely culprit. Finn continued questioning to get the woman's name, though Tomas likely already had it. I could hear them through the comms as I wandered.

Where along Park Avenue had George been attacked, and how far did he coast before coming to a stop at the porch?

The shadows were growing long, and the air had cooled. We had learned little from this scene, and it would be night soon. We still could hit up a few more witnesses from the deli, but I doubted any of them would turn out not to have been there and indicate an intentional ruse. The dwarf supposition seemed less likely than before. Standing under a tree that grew beside the sidewalk, my mind wandered to David and Marie; their attack proved the most personal, and perhaps the key.

"Kristen?" Finn asked over the comms. He strode toward me.

I waited for him to arrive. The comms were keyed so they wouldn't echo our words as we got close to each other. "How far would he coast? George Dillon, that is." I gestured toward an oncoming car. "Thirty, forty, or more miles per hour. If he'd veered off at this tree, he would have scraped against it, or the curb. I don't see any evidence of that."

Finn studied Park Avenue and the intersection before the house. "Maybe already slowing to take the corner? Tomas, do we have any idea where George Dillon was driving to? Home? Work?"

Tomas swore. "Do you even look at your emails? Officers called his job at the pharmacy. He'd been heading to lunch. They don't know where."

"Maybe he has a girlfriend." David sounded better. "Best use of a lunch hour."

Finn cocked his head. "Tomas, do we have any known associates in this direction?"

"Not yet. I'm still running through all his social connections, though."

"Tomas, do we have any connections between witnesses?" I asked.

"Of course. Emily Brown and Xavier Vasquez from the first scene. The deli has numerous connections within the staff, pairs eating together, a couple in line. They cross with the employee victim, especially within staff. George Dillon doesn't show up against the deli staff, though. I'll plot it out and email it to everyone. Check your damned emails."

The mention of Xavier made me cringe. His life and the boy's were upside down at the moment. We could have handled that better.

Finn nudged his head to our car. "I don't think we can get any more from this scene. Tomas, I don't see any cameras near here."

I glanced around us, especially up toward the direction the vehicle had come from. There was just a small parking lot and the end of the wide median on that side of the intersection. "Maybe the house on the corner?" I pointed across the street. There were no cars parked there or at the house farther down.

Finn shook his head, causing his dreads to dance. "Maybe later. We need to get through a couple more interviews to make sure we didn't have a doppelganger at the deli. We'll stay the night and start up again in the morning."

It hadn't been hot, and we'd spent most of the time in the air conditioning, but I'd be happy for a shower. I tried not to consider our upcoming interviews a waste, though I didn't believe they'd lead to anything. After the initial interviews, I'd suggest we revisit the first scene. It might offer me a chance to see something else, now that we'd had two more deaths.

David's voice popped into our comms with cheer. "Hey folks. All cleared to come join you tomorrow. I know you've missed me."

I had. We could use the help as well. "Bite and early?" I asked.

TWELVE

After plowing through three more interviews, we finally headed to the hotel Tomas had booked for us. The Tallahassee streets had quieted where we drove. Trees covered much of the city, filtering the street-lights. Our search hadn't yielded any results or new information, as I feared. I kicked my shoes off during the ride and wiggled my toes.

Tomas ran through the reports after quickly chastising that most had been emailed. "I've got four dwarves in Tallahassee, though none with residences or work within five miles of your zone of activity along Park Avenue. Two mer, and both of those are working at colleges. All six cryptids can be cleared with their activities during at least one incident. If it's merfolk or dwarf, then it isn't one of those residents." With his high pitch, he pronounced merfolk slightly off my use of their name. "Three arcane users live within a mile of the zone, and I've cleared them by activity as well. I've run Kristen's matrix of interconnectivity with only a couple unusual results. Read the email."

Finn pulled to a stop, waiting at the red light. "So a

visiting merfolk, dwarf or arcane user, or someone with Mahakala's Quartz."

"Who suddenly decided to start using it, or who has recently come to acquire it." Marie spoke more vibrantly than she had earlier in the day. She'd been quiet through our interviews.

"Have we checked our counterparts in Europe, Africa, and the others? Maybe the person who possesses it has been active but not in our radar." Finn asked.

Marie sighed. "I've been dealing with Stacey, who's been in a mood, and gotten nothing beyond what we have in reports. However, I'd say that's not an issue."

Finn turned us left. "How is Stacey?"

"A ray of golden sunshine." Marie swore.

"She even came to share a scowl with me," David said. "I think she likes me, but I don't date werewolves. I have my standards."

"With that, I'm on break. I'll check emails every couple hours, and my phone's active." Tomas sounded almost cheerful.

"David, get some rest," Marie said. "Finn, Kristen, check in with me in the morning."

Comms went quiet, and Finn tapped his, so I shut mine off. "Counterparts in other regions? How many are there?" I asked.

"Five regions. There's some duplication with each." Finn turned onto the last leg to our hotel at my gesture from the map. "Stacey handles the communication with her peers in each of them, but we get daily reports for Tomas to catalog and compare to any relevant activity. Stacey also deals with any immigrations or returns with dwarves and merfolk into our region, and the Consociation sends those reports to Tomas as well."

"Well, from his last report, I'd guess we're dealing with

the crystal. We just need to clear the last four from the deli and the one witness from today. I'd guess we're dealing with an innocent who lives near the Park Avenue stretch. Marie and David are the only ones that haven't occurred within a three-block concentration."

"Agreed. You wanted to revisit the first death?"

"Yes." I gestured to the right. "About a thousand feet. I'm hoping to jog something there, now that we have new incidents. I've found it useful in the past." I'd call Jade from the hotel. She still would be nervous, though our present case had no connection to Tarus. It still boggled my brain to think that I technically worked for the Consociation, but couldn't tell a soul. "David recovered quickly."

"He always does, if he gets human blood."

"What does Marie need to get back up on her feet?"

"Time. I've never seen her this damaged. I don't want to ask."

"How does she heal?" Vampires used their connection to Tarus, and werewolves their shifting, though werewolves were far more vulnerable. Our coven's grimoires had little information on dragon-shifters.

Finn tilted his head, bouncing his dreads. "She doesn't talk much about it, but from what I've gleaned it is different. Her presence here is an extension of her physical body, like poking a finger into another realm. It's a cognizant digit though, fully aware and not connected spatially." He pulled into the hotel parking lot, searching for a space. "Healing is through a replacement process from the main body."

"Like blood flowing from the core to a bruised finger?"

"Let's say yes. It takes a while for the transfer to have an effect. I worried once that she might die or disappear. She has, according to the archives."

I blinked. "Marie died?"

"During the wars. She said the damage was too severe and she needed to restore in her home realm, Salmhalla. It supposedly takes effort to shift into another realm." Finn pulled into a parking space and turned off the engine, facing me. "I wouldn't worry about her at this point. I just can't give you a time frame. She's obviously well enough to intercede with Stacey."

We exited where the air smelled clear and fragrant with nearby blooming flowers. Spring had arrived in full force in Tallahassee. Pulling out my go bag, I wished I'd brought a small steamer for my shirt and slacks. This long packed, they'd be wrinkled. I spoke as I juggled the weight. "I'm still a bit lost on the mechanics, but then I never fully understood how vampires and werewolves draw from their realm, either."

"Tomas has scientific studies dating back to the 1920s on that process, though I'm not versed in it." He slung the rifle bag over his shoulder, and I winced at the potential reaction from the hotel staff.

"Well, I'll add it to my to-be-read list. That's growing rather long." I closed the car door and motioned to his weapon. "That doesn't raise an eyebrow or two?"

Finn grinned. "Always."

Fifteen minutes later I used a lifting spell from the Mer realm to throw my bag onto the bed and started stripping out of my suit. I hung the jacket while running through the remaining witnesses. We'd hit the couple living together and would have to track most of the singles down at their jobs, I imagined.

Tomas had a wife and kids, but always seemed to be ready for us by the time Finn woke up. Marie would still be in her office, and I had to wonder if she had her own place, or lived at the FBI headquarters. Why not? Had David gone home?

I unzipped my go bag and yanked out my water bottle with another spell from Mer. I'd be sleeping soon, so I didn't care if using magic fatigued me. Lifting spells didn't have a true tactile response, but I could tell resistance to movement enough to wrap around something and hold it. Of all my craft, being lazy and picking up things with Mer was my shining accomplishment. All spells were an extension of our consciousness, so we had a sense of where they were. A warning ward off the Dur-Alf realm could be triggered anywhere in the world, and we'd know it.

I left the shower steaming my shirt and slacks for the next day, peeled open a protein bar, and sat with my water in an oversized T-shirt. Dialing Jade, I chewed quickly.

"Hi, Honey."

"Are you okay?" I almost heard mom at the end of her sentence.

"I am, Honey. My work is dangerous, but I'm very careful."

"If you don't change something, it will happen."

I sighed, resting my protein bar on its wrapper and brushing off my fingers. "We both know that we can't predict what change would affect it." Researching with seers outside my coven, I knew more than my ex-husband Anthony or even my mother, Sorrel. Perhaps my grandmother might have had more extensive knowledge, but we'd never talked about it. "But forewarned is forearmed. Next time I'm anywhere near Tarus, I'll be exceptionally careful."

Jade remained quiet; at least she wasn't crying.

I changed the subject. "I'm down in Tallahassee where it's warm and all spring flowers. Still cold up there?" I asked the usual questions; next would be about summer break. This year, I'd take a couple days and do it.

"Not bad," she said.

"Summer break. You sent me the dates. I'll look for time in June. We could drive up to the Canadian border." She preferred the more isolated places.

"You're just going to ignore this?" Jade asked. Her tone had a bite to it.

"Not at all. I just don't want you to be upset about it. I'm concerned, take my word for it." Jade's visions had come true, and when they hadn't, we could usually track it to a change in the person's life. Most of her ability focused on people she knew. A lot of it was good news. We kept those secret, and she found joy when they unfolded.

We fumbled through a little more conversation, then I let her go. An empty spot opened in my chest, and I forced myself not to think of the distance I'd placed between us. What kind of mother did that?

I finished my snack and water before brushing my hair. I'd learned more about the Consociation today. Dragon-shifters still eluded me, but Marie had a daughter with some impressive powers. We'd pissed off Investigator Dee, but cleared the path for our investigation. I grabbed my phone to log into Tomas's email and found one from Udy with an autopsy that didn't surprise me. Sally's vertebrae had severed her spinal cord, so she'd died painlessly.

I grimaced reading through it and finally put the cell on a charger by the bed. Turning off the lights with a lifting spell, I climbed under the covers. Finn liked to get up early, so I set my alarm for six. At least the hotel had a breakfast bar downstairs and a coffee maker in the room.

Hours later, my alarm went off in the middle of a horrible dream born from Jade's prediction, and I easily pried myself out of bed. The room had chilled, and I fumbled with my magic to turn on lights. For a minute I sat, wading out of the nightmare and back into our plans for the day. I absently checked my email, relieved that

Tomas hadn't started already. He waited for me to make coffee, and when I came back stacked them one after the other.

I'd already gone through all my emails when Finn called. "Room service breakfast? I'd like to chat about our plan for the morning. I've added a couple people to talk to."

"Sure." I hoped the cheese omelet was on the in-room menu. I'd wiped out the creamer and had been about ready to head downstairs. "Now?"

"If you're ready."

Suit and holster on, I had my go bag packed, but left it at the door. Finn appeared as ready when he let me into his room. He waved a card at me. "Not much on the menu."

I smiled at the make-your-own omelet. "Works."

Like mine, his room had a small round table and two chairs, where we sat after making the call downstairs. The room smelled like the lotion Finn used on his dreads. He leaned back, lightly tapping on the table. "Tomas never got through to the deli manager, so we'll catch him at work."

"I'd like to see the layout anyway."

"Agreed. I'd like to catch him last, if Tomas can line up the others beforehand. One got into work around eight. Another was a little after that."

"Well, we can do a walk-through on the first scene while we're at the deli," I said.

"Depending on David's schedule, maybe we can meet him there."

"When is his flight?"

Finn shrugged. "He's not an early riser on a good day."

Hungry, I glanced at the door. "Who were the others you wanted to add in today?"

"Three witches who live in the area and cross-referenced with the deli. Tomas pulled up the transactions.

They weren't at the deli during any of the time frames. I'm going to want to do them alone." He tapped his chest where I guessed he'd placed Yan's Pin.

I nodded, not liking to be left out. "I'll sit in the car on comms. Do you think a witch is involved? I've never known a witch who could interact with our realm."

"It's been done. The last we have in the database died in Russia where she lived to about a hundred and twelve. Prior to that, there were other cases, but the records are flimsy. I wouldn't put it past Iliodor."

"How do they do it? Can they see it? I didn't see anything when Herta used Earth realm magic on me, not really."

"Vague notes lead us to believe they do." He raised one shoulder in a shrug. "The dwarves and merfolk do. We assume some witches have enough craft to use it. We have two arcane rituals out of Egypt which utilize the Earth realm. Obviously a couple talismans."

"I know Yan's Pin was formed with the Earth Realm. There are others? I haven't been back to the database since all this started."

"Mahakala's Quartz." He paused long enough for me to offer a sheepish grimace; I'd known that. "Use any future downtime digging through what you can in Tomas's archives, rather than letting Stacey goad you into the cold cases. I'm not saying they're not important to review, though."

I flushed at the reminder of my folly. However, I did have some quick research I wanted to do regarding the rave massacre. After we finished here, Tomas could pull me some data. Joe Capra had been useful, and the case intrigued me. At least Marie was back, even if just on comms. David would join us today, and having some of the team reunited would make it feel more complete. I was proud of the ease in which I'd been assimilated; it helped alleviate some of my concerns of being an inexperienced outsider.

I jumped when someone rapped at the hotel room door, then smiled as my stomach grumbled. A solid meal, and I'd be ready to tackle the morning's interviews.

CHAPTER

THIRTEEN

"I don't remember anyone outside," said our latest witness, a secretary with straight black hair working at a law firm. Her dark eyes made me think of Cleopatra. "And I was out there the moment I saw that poor girl's body." She made a face as if she stifled a gag, then shivered. "Likely I would have had to run into someone to notice them. Sorry."

Both Finn and I had shaken her hand; she wasn't a dwarf in disguise, and from her recall of the event, she paid attention to nothing. Only one witness might have seen someone coming toward the door, but he remembered movement, not even a shape. I guessed we'd be on our way to search out Finn's witches. Tomas had cleared one who had been in Pensacola until last night.

"If you remember anything else." Finn handed the woman Tomas's card. I needed some of those.

As we stepped out of the office into the warming Tallahassee air, I pulled up my phone to find our next destination. It was lunch time, but the heavy breakfast kept me from being too hungry. "Are we picking up David?"

We passed bright purple azaleas without catching a scent, but the bees buzzed happily. "We'll see when he arrives. We've got at least an hour."

"Well, it's fifteen minutes to our next stop, so I thought we might be done in time to swing in that direction."

"That works." Dreads dangled over his left eye as he peered back at me. "Remember, you're in the car."

"I haven't forgotten. Not that I like it."

Inside the car, the heat had built up, and the air freshener stunk. It didn't resemble pine at this point. "What if it's a mundane using the arcane ritual you mentioned? We haven't explored that possibility because we're focused on Mahakala's Quartz. Could we get a dwarf or merfolk to sniff around like David did for Tarus?"

Tomas swore on the comms. "Merfolk don't sniff around like some canine."

I grimaced and pressed my fingers to my lips. "Sorry." Tomas could be so silent that I'd forget he was always listening.

Finn laughed silently, starting the engine. "Kristen didn't mean anything by it, Tomas. However, would it be possible?"

There was silence on the comms as I pointed Finn to our left and we exited the parking lot. Finally, Tomas spoke. "Possible, yes. Find a dwarf."

Mimicking a chagrined expression, I drank my water quietly.

Marie came on the comms for the first time since Finn had detailed our plans for the day. "Tomas, send a request to the Consociation. We don't have to be on site unless they find something. Good idea, Kristen."

My eyebrows shot up and I peered at Finn, who winked. Smiling, I pointed our directions at the next intersection.

"Any word on Leah, Tomas?" Marie asked.

"She's on a transatlantic flight now. ETA to Tallahassee 11:14 a.m. tomorrow. Stacey nixed the expedite."

"Of course. Keep me updated."

"Leah?" I mouthed to Finn.

He smiled and spoke loud enough for the comms to pick it up. "Leah's helped us out before. She's been working on cases in Europe for the past three months."

I'd ask more later, when we weren't on comms. We drove down a larger thoroughfare which had two lanes and Tallahassee's constant greenery between one and two-story buildings. Traffic bustled, and the scent of exhaust drew in along with the cool air conditioning. My grin remained as we slowed for cars turning off at side streets. Both Finn and Marie had appeared pleased with my thought, and in truth, I'd almost not mentioned it. Wards usually faded quickly if not immediately after use, and there were logistic issues considering the space behind the deli counter.

Tomas interrupted my meanderings. "I've got an accident on Franklin and Park. In your zone. Two cars. Local enforcement in route."

"We're on Franklin Boulevard, heading north. We just passed College Ave.," I said.

"The right direction, then." Tomas sounded curt, or I could have still been embarrassed.

"Any reports to indicate this is our case?" asked Finn.

"I'm tracking keywords, but the calls came into the station just before I informed you. Nothing mentioned other than an accident. Cams show only one driver has exited their vehicle. Running both plates."

"There." Traffic bunched ahead of us where two men walked in the intersection, just heads at this distance.

Hemmed in with a grassy median and curb, Finn slowed sharply and yanked the car into someone's driveway. He barely threw it into park before his buckle clanked open. "Stay here," he said.

I unbuckled and opened my door as he did. "There are civilians clustered at the intersection. They're in as much danger as I am." He could order me to stay, and I might.

Finn glared, then tilted his head to follow. His dreads bounced as he ran. He already had a good lead. I locked the doors and raced after him.

The two men were at the door of a small blue sedan and appeared to be talking to the driver through a shattered window. More people had opened their doors and stood to see over the cars ahead. Some jerk in a black pickup truck wove through the intersection to continue down Park Avenue.

From the position of the cars, a now empty gray SUV had been coming from our direction along Franklin, and the blue sedan had been heading east on Park Avenue, along the same path and a block down from the last accident. The SUV hid the back of the sedan where it had impacted. The front end of the blue car and driver were visible. My pulse rose in apprehension more than exertion.

Sirens sounded in the distance. Marie and Tomas were silent on the comms, so I could hear Finn call out, "FBI," as he approached. "Back it up a bit, but don't leave the scene. EMTs are on the way."

I dodged around a man who swore and hopped out of the passenger door of a pickup, jumping to the sidewalk. The last curse might have been for me. A little late, I slowed and pulled out my phone, taking a video of the last few cars I passed before reaching the intersection. I had their plates and some faces if they left the scene.

"Can you speak?" asked Finn over the comms.

I glanced up and found him leaning into the car. A woman had paused on the sidewalk with her dog, so I took a video of her. The traffic lights had cameras. We'd have more witnesses, or suspects, at this accident than any other. The sirens wailed closer, coming up Franklin as we had.

The man in the car didn't respond, leaning against his steering wheel and door. His eyes blinked, staring at Finn. Cars had lined up along eastbound Park Avenue, so I brought my phone up and videoed them. Angry faces glared at me, and I hoped none of them had a crystal in their pocket.

"Local FBI ETA thirteen minutes." Tomas's high-pitched comment overran a softer, comforting statement from Finn to the victim.

"Driver appears alive and alert," I said. Maybe this wasn't our case. We'd know when the EMTs tried to move him. "Is there anything we can do to help?"

Marie spoke in the comms. "No. The EMTs will assume neck injury and brace before they move him. It might save him from being killed, but the move to a back board might still sever his lower spinal cord. There's nothing we can do but warn them, and Tomas has already done that. We've got you on the traffic cams."

I glanced up at the camera dangling above, imagining Tomas's room with twelve screens lining the walls up to the ceiling. Did Marie still float in her office?

Honking, an ambulance drove the wrong way along Franklin, avoiding the line of cars. Some had already backed up and were attempting to turn around. I moved to the entwined cars to make room for the emergency vehicle.

The SUV had left skid marks, trying to stop. There were none for the driver of the car traveling down Park Avenue. Had he had the right of way, or couldn't he move to brake? Finn glanced over the top of the blue sedan as I came into view.

The driver's left shoulder was pressed against the

window. A pale blue shirt wrinkled with pressure at his shoulders. His short brown hair covered the top left of the steering wheel he rested against. In any other circumstance, I'd think he was a drunk who had fallen asleep in his car. No bones protruded into his shirt. The skin on his face wasn't mottled or bruised yet.

The ambulance pulled around the SUV and parked a dozen feet from where I stood. "Ours, or local EMTs?"

"Local," Tomas said. "I got the calls a minute after they hit 911, not before."

Finn had resumed his position. "Hold on there, Buddy. Help's on the way."

I walked around the hood, and the man's eyes flicked to follow me. The right side of his face was an angry red, with tinges of purple at the jaw. It might be our case, or those injuries could be from the crash.

A female EMT with pale skin jumped out of the passenger side and peered at me. I flashed my FBI badge, but she just turned for the rear of their vehicle.

The black man who strode from the driver's door rounded the front of the ambulance and focused on me. "Is this the man who might have brittle bone disease?"

"Yes." I hoped I didn't sound surprised.

He ignored me after that, peering in at the man who watched me and Finn. The driver winced, and even that movement appeared to pain him. Perhaps he had been attacked. My chest tightened. The next move could kill him. I scanned around us, half expecting someone to be lurking in the bushes, watching us. Police had arrived and were setting up their cars to block traffic or reroute it.

Finn pulled back to my position, looking through the cracked windshield. The side of the car was crumpled from the rear quarter panel into the front of the SUV. The windows had been blown into the seats and driver. The wounded man kept his eyes on us until the woman pried open the passenger door and crawled in with a neck brace.

I winced, unsure if his bones could take any pressure. An expression of terror and pain shot across his face, his lips moving as if whispering.

"Hey, where's the party?" David's voice on the comms jolted me.

"Stow it, David. They're at a scene. Tomas has a taxi waiting for you." Marie kept her voice low and calm.

"A taxi? Did they at least wipe the vomit off the back seat?"

"Stow it. Tomas gave the driver the location."

With the female EMT in the front seat, the man opened the driver's door. Panic widened the victim's eyes and his nostrils flared. His left arm and shoulder didn't snap when they leaned him back, and I sighed some relief that this might not be our case.

"Ben Williams according to the license plate. I've got a photo match with his face now," Tomas said. I didn't glance at the traffic camera to determine how he got the angle to work.

I moved to the front corner to see the male EMT shift the left arm without any difficulty. When the woman shifted the victim's right arm though, I heard the snap. She cringed and I saw the driver pass out.

More bones broke as they moved him to the gurney. His right leg bled through his pale jeans. "His left side is fine," I said.

Finn bobbed his head. "Yeah. Noticed."

"This isn't as bad as the others. Maybe the effect is ranged." I hadn't considered it possible, but my lifting spells faltered at distance, and they had weight limitations. "Just the closer side affected perhaps."

"A good hypothesis. Earth realm healing is best at

contact, weakens at range." Tomas had just complimented me, and I had to turn to Finn with my eyebrows raised. "Local FBI on scene. SSA Szinsky."

Finn spun slowly, then strode off toward Franklin where the traffic had disappeared and a barricade had replaced them. Two black SUVs were pulling up. We'd confirmed the accident was our case and possibly lost some witnesses. I peered up Park Avenue where a police car blocked the road right at the intersection where our last accident had been. Ben Williams's attack would not have been witnessed at this intersection, but farther up the road.

Finn had begun introducing himself to the local FBI, and I spoke lightly. "Heading up Park." As I walked, I sent Tomas the videos of the scene so he could pull out potential witnesses.

The midday heat had gotten warmer than yesterday. Sweat already gathered around my chest and armpits. The scent of blossoms and growth mixed with light exhaust. I stepped onto the sidewalk on the south edge of Park Avenue where the accident had been and Williams's right side would have been closest. Over the comms, Tomas and Finn coordinated with the local FBI to retrieve witnesses.

Park Avenue inclined slowly then rose up a fair distance away. The road was two-way here. "Tomas, how far to the other crash site?"

"Two hundred and fifteen meters."

I strolled on the mismatched sidewalk in front of a two-story brick house. The officer directing the detour noticed me, then continued to divert eastbound traffic to a side street across from me. How far would Ben Williams have coasted?

Finn had begun interviewing the two men who had been at the scene when we arrived. One was the driver of the SUV who swore he had a green light, and the other was a resident who heard the crash. They didn't see any other witnesses except the cars following the SUV. I had those license plates. They didn't remember any pedestrians.

They wouldn't since the attack would have happened farther up the road, unless Ben Williams made a habit of running red lights. Reaching the next house, I turned and studied the distance from the driveway to the intersection.

"Tomas, can you confirm if Ben Williams had a red light?"

"He did."

At thirty or forty miles per hour, Williams would still be moving quickly downhill to where the accident occurred, fast enough that the SUV couldn't stop in time. I waved back toward the intersection. "Can you see me, Tomas, on Park Avenue?"

He swore. "Yeah, you're the blurry idiot waving in the street."

I stopped and pursed my lips. "Could you please rewind and watch Ben Williams driving down this road before the accident?"

"Turns left from Beverly Court onto Park Avenue." Of course he'd already watched the videos.

The officer waved a gawking driver in a pickup to turn down the side street. I stepped off the sidewalk to cross to the other side.

Tomas swore quietly. "Ben Williams nearly pulls into traffic, then stops sharply when a west bound car swerves around his bumper. I can't see him clearly, but I'd guess he was agitated. He might have thrown something out of his passenger window."

Veering my path to the back of the police car, I focused on an empty fast-food cup and an obvious wet discoloration. Two fresh skids marked the road at the stop sign.

The officer glanced at me, and I showed him my badge. I circled and headed for the closest building, which happened to be a two-story white business on the northeast corner. Faded, rusted, and decorated with leaves, it had a sign on the Park Avenue frontage.

"Tomas, do you see any pedestrians when Ben Williams has his near collision?"

"Too distant to identify, but yes, west of the cross street in the shade. They're stopped and watching."

The building was an office for some educational association. In Atlanta, there were security cameras on nearly every building, but few here in Tallahassee. I walked up faded stairs onto the creaking porch and tried the door. The air was freezing inside. A tinge of moldy carpet fought with a floral air freshener, and old wood-paneled walls had been painted a decade ago. From where an older woman sat behind a plain wooden desk, she smiled, slightly surprised at my arrival. I would have sworn the furniture came from the front of a classroom.

"Excuse me, I'm Agent Winters of the FBI." I showed her my badge, and her eyes widened. "Did you happen to hear a commotion in the intersection outside your door about half an hour ago? Maybe more?"

Her face softened and she bobbed her head in a nod. "They do it all the time. However, yes, just around lunch I did hear someone slam on their brakes. Of course, they had to lean on their horn, because it's always someone else's fault. I couldn't hear his words, but from the tone I imagine they weren't very nice." She frowned. "Was someone hurt?"

"Not here. You don't have any security cameras, do you?"

She motioned to the sparse waiting room. "Not much need."

I stepped back into the heat without much more information than I'd started with on my trek down Park Avenue. The officer motioned to a box truck on Beverly. "Tomas, can you rewind back to get a facial recognition on the pedestrian?"

"Nope. Tried. They come to Park from Beverly and cut across the parking lot. Ninety-two percent probability on female."

Across the street from me, a pitted, half-sand parking lot in front of a small apartment building had entrances both on Beverly Court and Park Avenue. It made for a shortcut for pedestrians, though one of the residents had blocked the closest entrance with a parked car. Flood lights adorned the upper floor's porch, but no cameras.

"What do you have, Kristen?" Finn asked over the comms.

I stepped to the corner, peering back to the intersection and flashing lights of the police. "Our driver might have been causing a disturbance. Screeching tires and honking horn. The first death had cursing and honking horns. The first vehicle accident had loud music. A disruption or fracas appears to be a recurring theme, except for Sally. I'd like to find out what made her different."

"David's here. We'll hit up the deli and manager. You can wait in the car, and we'll drop you at the hotel afterward."

My cheeks flushed and my chest tightened. I knew Finn excluded me for my own safety, but it still bothered me, like I wasn't a part of the team.

FOURTEEN

"On my way," I replied to Finn over the comms before I crossed the blocked street. My back straightened as I walked downhill to the accident. My emotions hollowed out my chest. David and Finn continuing without me was no different than sitting on my thumbs while SWAT took the lead, but with a new team, it didn't feel the same.

As I returned, Finn was listing the witnesses he wanted to interview with David. A tow truck had arrived, flashing dull orange among the blue and red.

Tomas spoke over the comms. "First witch on your list is back from lunch. She's a mortgage agent and at her office. You have the link in an email from this morning."

I just listened. The first day on the team I had expected the investigation to go like this, with me on the outside looking in. An officer in the intersection studied me with a hint of hostility, perhaps a friend of Investigator Dee.

David appeared as well dressed and in as good health as he'd been the day of the attack on him and Marie. He and Finn stood in the shade of a tree overhanging the far sidewalk. The local FBI were talking beside their black SUVs, peering at me when I crossed behind the two entangled vehicles. The ambulance was gone.

At David's feet were a blue igloo cooler and his dark go bag. He drank through a straw from a foil juice pouch. Spotting me, he posed with his arms outstretched and a toothy grin on his handsome face. "I'm back. Hopefully I didn't ruin my chances with Lindsey, if we end up here tonight."

"You seem better." The sight of his cooler made me thirsty.

He lifted his juice pouch in salute. "Doc's orders."

I cringed, my nose wrinkling as I spoke in a quiet voice. "Blood?"

David raised his finger to his lips, then peeked at the FBI agents. "Shh. Everyone will want some. I'm willing to share one or two, for friends."

I carefully focused on Finn, ignoring David's antics. "I think the attacks have to do with disturbances. The only one that doesn't fit is Sally. We need to try harder with the manager."

"He's next. I'm sorry about pulling you from the action." Finn did appear regretful.

"I'm not," Marie said over the comms. "I'll not have an unprotected asset risked if it can be avoided. We have a choice in this case. By my count, you've got a lot of interviews, Finn. Move it."

My lips pursed, but I understood her concerns. At least she didn't consider me expendable. I stopped when my hand started tugging at my curls.

As I moved to pass David and head for the car, he pointed at the blue cooler. "Lend a hand?"

"Sure." I picked up his go bag, surprised at the weight.

Finn grabbed it from me and led the way back down

Franklin to the car. "I'll try to park where you have sight of the deli. No promises."

David passed me, sucking on his foil pouch and swinging his cooler. Cones blocked the street where we'd left our car. The sun angled to our right into early afternoon, and the heat rose as we exited the shade.

"Tomas, how much time do we have before the deli closes?" I asked.

"Over an hour."

When Finn unlocked the car, David opened the back door. I thought for a moment he would take the rear seat; instead, he put his cooler on the floor, tossed his empty container inside, and pulled out a fresh pouch. As he slid into the front, I circled around to the driver's side; I wasn't moving the cooler.

We backed out, turned around, and headed down a side street. Finn tapped on his wheel. "First the deli, drop off Kristen, witches, and then Tomas will have a list for us from the latest attack. Kristen, I agree that this might be someone reacting to a disturbance. We need to find an overlap. Dig into that with Tomas while you're at the hotel."

I hated the idea of sitting in the hotel room. "Leave me in the car — rear seat. I can be back up during the rest of these interviews."

Finn's dreads swung as he moved to glance at me in the mirror. "Sorry. We haven't cleared the manager with an interview at his home yet. I've got David. It's not worth the risk."

We turned onto Monroe Street where the deli was, and I tried not to focus on my worth. David sipped silently on his pouch. Finn pulled into a parking spot on the opposite side of the street from the deli where I could see part of the front. A dark blue truck on lifts with oversized tires was parked in front of the restaurant, blocking some of my view. It wasn't the best vantage. He hadn't opted for the space two cars ahead nearly across from the deli.

"Stay in the car." Finn left the engine running.

"Let me grab my bag from the trunk." I opened my door and he nodded.

David climbed out, wincing at the sun. "I can share." He wiggled his drink as he might his mints. I suddenly wondered if they were regular mints, or something else.

"Pass." I would never be accepting one of his mints.

I dallied getting my bag long enough to watch them cross the street and approach the store before I had to climb in the car. A bell rang in my comms as they opened the deli door.

"Mr. Bebelle, I'm SSA Billings. This is Special Agent McCree. We wanted to talk with you about the incident involving your employee, Sally Oswald. We haven't been able to contact you." Finn's amiable tone grew louder as he spoke. "Sir?"

The reply over the comms sounded distant and gruff. "Already talked to the police."

David's tone had a playful air to it. "Wow, look at this roast beef. It's so rare."

The gruff voice of the manager came closer. "You can't go in there. Don't touch that."

"Actually, Mr. Bebelle, this is still a crime scene. We haven't released it." Finn sounded annoyed, possibly with David. "Still, Agent McCree should probably not be back there."

"Just a slice." David hummed.

"Fine." The manager was close. "What do you need to know?"

"Was anyone upset at the time Sally died, or just before?" Finn asked.

"No. No more than usual when they're waiting in line. Everybody's in a hurry at lunchtime." The manager had moved away, fading, so I cupped my hand over my ear and comms, drowning out a passing car.

"Where were you when she collapsed?"

The manager sighed. "Back here at the end of the line, behind the tea. I'd brought a sleeve of large cups from the stock room. We were busy. Sally was two yards from me, backing out an order from the register, then she just dropped. She was one of my best."

Finn didn't speak immediately. "Mr. Bebelle, did you see anyone outside the window? There?"

Close to the comms, I could hear the manager snort. "Why would I be looking out there with her dropping on the floor like that? I don't have time for your nonsense. James is right about you folks. I should call him in here now."

"That's your choice, of course." Finn's tone was cool, but congenial. "I would have assumed you'd be concerned about Sally, and why she'd died like that."

"James said pregnant women get bad bones. It was horrible, but nothing that would affect my customers. Still lost a day's business."

I stiffened at his comment and tone, as if he blamed Sally for dying and ruining his sales. Some monsters didn't need magic to hide. Surely he knew about the man who died outside his store. If he weren't so greedy, perhaps he'd be worried for his own health.

Finn and David dawdled with the man while I steamed over his merciless attitude and for my impending quarantine at the hotel. If the manager had seen anything unusual, he was in no mood to tolerate or help us as he curtly answered the last questions. We'd gained nothing from the interview. I thought he might throw David out over the second slice of roast beef.

Eating Parmesan crisps, I watched Finn and David emerge to head back to the car. Clouds had moved in and shaded the street. My next stop would be a boring hotel room. "Marie?"

"Yes, Kristen."

"I'd like to requisition a small tablet for my go bag. It would help when I get stuck at the extended stay." I was being a little cocky, but she'd likely say no anyway.

"Situations like this will be rare. Finn can lend you the laptop." She sounded amused, rather than annoyed.

The offer didn't brighten my mood. I stuffed a cracker into my mouth to stave off a snarky remark suggesting I just head back to Atlanta. My quick comments often got me deeper into an argument than I intended, especially when I felt pushed aside. My mother had tolerated my behavior, but it had led to nasty arguments with my ex. Dealing with Jade's teenage retreat from conversation had helped me learn when to keep silent.

Finn opened his car door. "You catch all that?"

Sally's death still did not fit into my hypothesis. "Yep."

He must have caught something in my tone. "Sorry about having to dump you at the hotel."

I took a moment as he started the car and prepared to pull into the street. "I'm not thrilled about it and don't necessarily agree. However, I'll try to be useful." Once in my time as detective, I'd been put on desk duty while they reviewed a shooting. That had been their procedure, and I'd taken it better.

Thirty minutes later, I tossed my go bag on my hotel bed and walked Finn's laptop to the desk. I peeked between the curtains at the gray sky. A storm was moving in. The room smelled clean, urging me to strip and shower after a day of mucking about in the heat. While my comms charged, I put on a fresh shirt and slacks.

I texted Tomas. "Comms off. Text or email." Obviously they could call, but I doubted they would. David and Finn were off to interview witches.

Pulling up our secure email, I found Tomas's last report on the witnesses. There was scant data on most, and many were marked with "assumed" and a reference to a license plate. I might have at least talked to the first couple drivers in the line and gotten their names and a statement. Finn had been with the driver; I could have been more useful gathering data instead of gawking.

"Stop it," I told myself, glad my comms were off. A talisman and David's innate constitution were a better match to this magic than my abilities.

I dug back through the email where Tomas outlined the connection, and realized the data was a live link. Tomas kept it updated, likely through a program. Emily and Xavier still showed as linked, along with a couple pairs from the diner's customers and Sally's connection with her co-workers.

Below were the expanded lists of witnesses and the witches Finn and David had left to interview. Residents of the apartment building were noted as present or not present. From either my video or traffic cams, license plates showed with names, some inside brackets. Emily's mystery man was at the bottom labeled "Cowboy" with question marks. I would have noticed a cowboy hat, and Tomas was likely on the lookout for it.

As I watched, the data shifted, and a bracketed name next to one of the license plates disappeared and a new name, Barry Weir, replaced it. Then the listing flashed red and disappeared from the list. "What the hell?" I reached for my phone, then sighed and pulled my comms off the charger.

I was going to ask Tomas about the name that had vanished off my list, but he was speaking. ". . . the son has a friend in the apartment next to Xavier's, *and* he's an arcane user."

Finn interrupted immediately. "I need an address for Barry."

Tomas's high pitch added to his tone of excitement. "Three degrees from Iliodor. I'm trying to track his movements during each of the incidents now. Home and work addresses sent to email, but I haven't verified where he's located presently. iPhone."

I scrolled to the top of my data and found the missing name connected to one of the people from the apartment. The two were above Emily and Xavier with a dotted line to each of them.

"Barry's next on your list, once Tomas has coordinates." Marie sounded like her old self.

Perhaps she'd be joining the rest of the team on interviews soon. This could be the piece we'd been searching for. My pulse sped at the thought of a fresh lead — but I'd be in the hotel. Yan could have made an earring for me while he was at it.

"Kristen, what are you working on?" Marie asked.

"Tomas built me a live set of connections. It just updated with his newest findings." *I'm not really* doing *anything*, I thought.

"Does that give you something?"

I glared at the screen. "Well, Xavier and Emily are connected, more than anyone else. They live near here, eat at the deli, and might know their neighbor's friends, or not."

"Not Xavier, obviously. Keep digging."

We'd eliminated Emily as much as anyone else, but she could still be a possibility, if she had been near the diner during Sally's attack. In the background of our comms, I heard a car door close and the muffled traffic.

"Tomas. Can you please track Emily's movements during the other attacks?"

"Emily's phone hasn't left her apartment since the first attack. She called Xavier multiple times without a connection and spoke twice to a Dale Brown."

"Her cousin. A picker according to her."

"I know her connection to Dale Brown." Tomas swore, continuing, "If she left her residence, she didn't take her phone. No one does that nowadays. I find no connection to any other witness or victim. She lives nearby, but many of the people on my list do."

There had to be someone I was missing, or Tomas had found the connection with Barry, this friend of Xavier's neighbors. Perhaps the mystery cowboy was an extremely adept dwarf or mer who could attack at a long enough range that we weren't pooling our witnesses from their location. What if Marie or David had been the target, and whoever had this ability kept killing, waiting for a chance to finish them off?

Thunder grumbled outside, and I checked the time. Too early for dinner.

The attacker had to be moving and likely drove to cover the entire range. Tomas would get hundreds of cars if I had him pull license plates from traffic cams within a multiple block radius during the time of each attack.

"Tomas, how many traffic cams cover the roads feeding into the intersections where we've had attacks?"

"You'd have to be more specific. Adjacent?"

"What if it's intentional, and they're picking random

targets from a distance. No nearby witnesses would matter."

Finn started speaking to their next witch, introducing themselves.

Tomas swore under his breath. "I get what you're aiming for. Let me see if I can write a program for a plate match."

I was about to thank Tomas when David spoke with his grandiose voice, and I imagined him flourishing a handsome smile. "Please, call me David. You've got a lovely apartment. Is that your roommate?"

I leaned back in the hotel chair and sent a lifting spell over to my water bottle. From the easy way it moved, I could tell it was nearly empty. As David played up his charisma with the witch, I stood, bringing the container into my hand. I listened half-heartedly even when Finn began asking relevant questions.

As I filled my bottle from the tap, Finn took their conversation into a private room. "We work for the Consociation," he said.

I stared at the running water, shocked.

"We need to know if you've seen any unusual activity or use of the realms lately in this neighborhood."

"No." As I would have been a month ago, the woman sounded terrified. No simple witch spoke to someone from the Consociation. "Like what?"

"Anything that might seem in the slightest unusual. Especially if you think they might be related to the craft, the arcane, or any of the realms." Finn sounded calm. I would never have guessed we would expose ourselves like that.

I ran back with my water and checked Tomas's emails for her data. She was twenty-three. Marie hadn't stopped Finn, so I gathered this was another tactic the team might use that I had no idea about. I would have been gaping like a fish if he'd done this in front of me.

They got nothing from the witch, though David did try for a number as he offered that he "might have some down time in Tallahassee."

As they left, Finn commented, "It's not her, or I'd be sending for someone to scrape David off the floor." He'd intentionally threatened her by using the Consociation. If she'd been hurting people, she'd see him as a threat, an enemy.

I sat in the hotel alternating between listening to Finn's interviews and plucking through any little piece of data. I kept coming back to the attacks being centered around disturbances. The deli had the most contained set of witnesses. I was missing someone. Perhaps a customer who had just left and found out their sandwich had pickles on it.

"Tomas, can you check a few of the transactions before Sally died to cross-reference against anyone we've interviewed — or a witness from the latest accident?"

"Running now." In the background of the comms, I could hear him crunching. "Not one cross-reference from that morning's credit card activity. Except a customer from lunch who also bought breakfast there." He swore. "Do you want me to add *all* these into your pool as well?"

I swallowed. "How about transactions ten minutes prior to Sally's death?"

"Four customers."

"Just those. Thank you."

Lightning flickered in the window and thunder sounded right behind it. The vengeful storm left background noise in our comms when Finn and David drove to their final interview of the evening.

"Any luck on Barry?" Marie asked.

Tomas snorted. "He's still going in and out of cell

range south of Tallahassee. It's a lot of swamp down there."

"What do you have for his location during the other attacks?"

"He's paranoid, so his phone doesn't track location. Cell towers put him in the zone of the attacks, but he could have been three blocks away."

"I don't let my phone track my location," I said.

"You don't have the wealth of conspiracy videos he has on his social media, nor do you subscribe to some of the darker forums that he does." Tomas sounded amused. "He does, however, like some of the Gamelit which you've read."

I frowned, but should have suspected that they'd dug into my life pretty deeply. *Goodreads* though?

"Kristen, room service, my room?" Finn asked as tires cut through rain-slick streets. "Give me fifteen to change."

"Sounds good." I finished my cooling tea and stuffed the empty bag of crisps into the garbage bin.

When Finn and David returned to the hotel, the storm had wrung itself of the worst of the rain. I'd been down to the desk for more tea and cream, and Barry had disappeared from Tomas's radar. When they cut their comms, I turned mine off and stuck it back in the charging case. Flicking lifting spells from the Mer realm, I tidied the room before heading over to Finn's.

They both were still wet, though Finn had changed into sweats for the evening and sat on his bed, menu in hand. His dreads swung as he peered under them with a nod.

David sipped on a pouch, stopping to pose for a handsome smile when I walked in. He sat in one of the chairs at the table. "I can't stay long. Meeting Lindsey down in

College Town." Even with his hair wet, it looked impeccable.

Finn tossed the menu to me, but I already planned on getting their mac and cheese. "I heard a little of what you were working on. Anything pan out?"

I knew their focus was on Barry. "I've gone down a few rabbit holes, but nothing has come from it. Tomas cross-referenced license plates during each incident from up to three blocks away and within a ten-minute time frame, but nothing there. He looked at some of the previous customers before Sally died, but none came up with any flags."

"We could add them to our list." Finn spoke, winced at the comment, then smiled. "Sorry. I know you want to be out there."

"I do." I tossed the menu on the bed. "I'm hungry."

David said. "Me too. I'll send your regards to Lindsey." He crumpled his empty pouch.

I mocked a frown, wrinkling my nose, but assumed he was just joking.

Finn remained on his bed, looking weary. "We're not getting any closer. I can hope this Barry is a lead, but I had my bet on Xavier as well. Does your gut tell you anything?" He pulled the phone to his lap, waiting for me to respond.

After being sidelined all day, it felt like a compliment, but this investigation seemed like a circus juggling act to me as well. "Well, the deli still bothers me."

Finn cocked his head. "What part?"

I shrugged and sat down at the table. "It's inside and contained, unlike all the others. We've dug through everyone in the room." Of all the scenarios, it fouled my conjecture of the attacks being responses to disturbances. "We are missing something." My lips tightened. "I'd like to go over there tomorrow, while you and David continue your interviews."

Finn took a deep breath. "Probably okay. We'll talk about it in the morning with Pyre." He dialed the number for room service.

CHAPTER

FIFTEEN

I woke in a foul mood from a disturbing dream I couldn't remember. I had tried to talk to Jade the night before, but she'd ghosted my call and then texted me she was out with friends. There was some comfort in her developing friends, and I hoped it wasn't a lie. The storm had come back to beat on my windows and even in the morning rain tapped on the glass.

Mostly, I didn't want to sit in this room another day.

I'd showered and was dressed by the time Finn called. "David and I are heading out. Tomas has a lead on Barry."

My chest hollowed. "Okay." I'd expected to at least talk about the case over breakfast, but they didn't need me. "Is it okay if I head to the deli?"

Finn's voice pulled back from the phone. "Pyre, are you okay with Kristen checking out the deli again?" Of course they were already on comms.

I whipped a lifting spell over to the charging case and plucked out my comms. Checking earlier would have been the better plan.

"That's what I thought. Wanted to check." Finn's voice became louder. "Keep in touch, but yes, feel free to check out the deli."

As he hung up, I put in my comms and tapped them on. I really only felt like a Danish this morning after eating so late. I ignored my mood and grabbed my key to go downstairs to the lobby for tea and a light breakfast.

The team discussed their plans for Barry as I walked down the hall and got in the elevator.

Tomas sounded excited. "I've got him heading through Crawfordville in the next ten minutes. If he continues north, the road is more isolated around an area called Leon Sinks. I'm sending you a coordinate where you should set up the barricade."

Marie spoke calmly. "I've got local FBI heading to 319 now. They'll wait at the coordinates for our call. David, you'll flag him down. Park the car a good hundred yards ahead of the FBI barricade. Finn, remain behind the car and have a clear shot. If David goes down, take the shot."

"Can I bring a lawn chair this time?" asked David. "Flopping to the asphalt ruined a perfectly good suit." I could hear the rain on the street in the background. They were already outside the hotel.

"If we had the time," Marie said.

I waited in the short line and ordered a cheese Danish and three-quarters of a cup of tea to leave room for the cream. Tomas rattled off logistics and timing of the local FBI, my team, and each time Barry's phone pinged a cell tower. I smiled at the server who handed me my order, even though I didn't feel it.

At a high-top table by the window I fixed my tea without thought, adding plenty of cream and sugar with automatic motions. I stared out at the rain and listened to my team tightening the noose on Barry Weir. The case might be done before I headed to the deli, and I tried to see that in a positive and selfless light.

I finished my breakfast and remained at the window until Finn arrived at their coordinates. I leaned forward, my hand over my ear.

"Lightning rod exiting the vehicle now, Pyre."

"Stow it, David."

Tomas spoke in a quick burst. "Three to four minutes out."

"The road is soaked. I'm going to ruin one of my best blazers."

"Pyre, I've got a truck coming at us. It's slowing down," Finn said.

"Tomas?" she asked.

"I've got Barry registered to a 1986 Chevy Malibu. Silver."

"Ooh," David sounded excited. "Tell me it's a wagon. I haven't seen one of them in a couple decades."

"David, check the truck. You've got a picture of Barry Weir. Finn, get it past you if you have time. Night storms. I don't need another casualty."

Tense, I patted at my curls which I'd been pressing to my ear. I could have hung back with the local FBI and at least been close to my team. In the background of the comms, I could hear an indistinct voice. Then Finn started the engine.

"Pyre, I think I see our target. The truck is moving past." Finn sounded preoccupied. The car turned off. "Repositioning." The door slammed shut, and Finn grunted. "He's stopping."

"No, come on, it's just little ole me." David's voice wavered, as if he were moving. "He's bolting, Pyre."

"Chase him down, Finn. Don't take a shot unless you know he's the cause of this."

David grunted, shoes slapping on wet asphalt. "In other words, when David drops."

I straightened, peering around the coffee shop. The line had disappeared, so I headed to the counter for more tea and cream. In the comms, the car started up and tires squealed into motion. The sound raised my pulse.

Finn screeched to a stop, David jumped in the car, and they were off again.

"Tea and creamer, please." I flashed a weak smile at the man behind the counter.

I nodded at their pleasantries as Finn raced the engine. His tires cut through water on the asphalt, though I didn't hear rain.

"Dammit. He's got a decent motor in that thing. I'm at ninety, Pyre."

"Finn, I can't set up a roadblock ahead. Local enforcement would man it, and we might lose them all. Stay with him."

"You've got an intersection a couple minutes away," Tomas said.

"Finn, do you have visual?"

"Affirmative. For the present. He's getting ahead of us. Almost a hundred now."

My hand holding the provided creamer and tea, I stood glazed at the counter. "Anything else, Ma'am?"

I jolted. "No, sorry."

As I turned for the hall leading to the elevators, Finn swore. "He just clipped a car. He was passing two of them, might have been on purpose. We've got a two-car accident here, Pyre." I could hear his engine slowing from its high pitch.

"Night storms." Marie sounded angry. "Tomas, find Barry Weir. Send the FBI up to assist Finn."

"It's bad. A truck rear-ended a Toyota and sent it into the gully. There could be injuries. I'm stopping."

In the background, I could hear someone yelling, possibly in pain. Another voice shouted, angry. A door slammed. The sounds of an argument grew closer to Finn's comms as I stepped into the elevator.

Pushing down frustration, I focused on what little I could do while Finn and David risked their lives. Detective work often included hours of quiet research. I would be focused on flushing out any leads we might have over-looked, and the deli would be my best bet. Meanwhile, I'd monitor the rest of my team's activities and check to see what reports Tomas had updated.

I could wait a little before I got a ride to the deli. Arriving at lunchtime might be my best option.

SIXTEEN

An hour after their failed attempt to apprehend Barry Weir, Finn and David returned to Tallahassee. Their suspect had disappeared off Tomas's radar. The team had a muted, defeated tone on the comms.

"Pyre, we're going to check Barry's residence, then back to our original list for the day." Finn's comms picked up the sound of rain pattering and the squeak of windshield wipers.

"Understood. Tomas is monitoring for Barry Weir. Be ready to disengage quickly and pursue."

I was left going through the data, searching for some missing piece other than Barry Weir. The weather had convinced me to wait before heading out to the deli. I'd prefer seeing their midday rush in action anyway. Tomas's programs would grind out any possible connection I could come up with, and they were failing miserably to bring me any leads.

As Finn and David resumed their interviews, they had little progress as most of their witnesses were at work this time of day, and conversations became brief with constant interruptions. The bulk of the witnesses had arrived after the accident and been stuck in the delay.

An hour before lunchtime, I checked in before calling for a ride. "Marie, Finn, I'm heading to the deli. I'm going to hang through lunchtime, maybe walk Park Avenue."

"Keep on comms," Marie said.

"Will do."

I tidied the hotel room and grabbed my mini umbrella before heading down to the lobby to wait. The street had rivulets of water running under the cars, though the actual rainfall had dropped to little more than a sprinkle.

By the time I reached the deli, it had stopped raining. The clouds left a gloomy threat above, but the air smelled clean. I tucked my umbrella in my jacket pocket and stepped carefully around puddles. My hair would still frizz from the weather, but I had a hair tie in my go bag.

"Hey." Investigator Dee stepped out of the diner, bag in hand. He wasn't wearing his uniform. "Haven't you bothered these people enough? They're just trying to move forward."

I thought of Sally's husband. He wouldn't be getting over this anytime soon. "Investigator Dee, I'm surprised to see you here." Gesturing to the bag, I asked, "What should I order?"

"He's not an investigator at the moment, he's under review," Marie said flatly.

The moment of sympathy that welled up quickly dispersed when he squared up to me, a hands-width from my chest. "Don't pull that BS on me. I damned well know what you're here for. I don't know what you people are up to, but I'd toss you out of Tallahassee if I could."

I moved to the side, aiming to go around him. "But you can't."

He adjusted to block me and stabbed a finger into my shoulder. "You have no idea what I'm capable of."

Stepping back, I studied his finger. I never appreciated machismo behavior, and had to take a calming breath. "I think you're *capable* of salvaging your career. However, it will come with some introspection on your part, such as where you lost control of your actions and your emotions. This moment is a good time to begin that lesson. I'll help by ignoring our little encounter here and moving on with my investigation and lunch." Pausing, I turned up to stare into his widening eyes. "Enjoy your sandwich."

He sputtered, but didn't stop me from walking to the door. I exhaled as the bell rang, announcing my entry above the chattering talk and rattle of a sheet pan. My pulse eased as I took another calming breath.

The restaurant smelled delicious with high notes of vinegar and toasted bread. The line extended along high glass cabinets up to the lower counter where an employee smiled at a customer. There was plenty of space for me to stand behind a young black woman wearing a halter top and jean shorts who spoke quietly on her phone. Four people waited ahead of her with one detailing their order. Behind the counter, I could make out three of the employees.

I ticked off the employee's names in my head, but really wanted to talk with the manager. As we stepped forward and the young woman ahead gave her order, I moved closer to the glass cabinet, hoping they'd be able to make a grilled cheese. I could sit here and eat, watching the midday business. The manager would be out at some point, and I'd catch him.

Finn and David were in the middle of an interview, and I listened half-heartedly as I scanned the restaurant.

David was making jokes for the sake of the woman, and she laughed at the worst of them.

A figure rose from one of the tables, empty plates in hand. My throat caught as he adjusted a wide-brimmed cowboy hat. He matched Emily's limited description of her mystery man. I opened my mouth to say something on the comms, then dug into my pocket. Tomas would need a picture to get facial recognition. He could match it against the register transactions, unless the man paid in cash.

He wore a dark purple shirt with lighter, decorative stitching on the upper chest and shoulders. Handsome, his pale skin, brown mustache, hat, and clothes made him appear to be someone who wished he were a cowboy.

As he moved, I snapped a hasty picture which I knew would be lousy. My pulse raced as he discarded his plates and turned to head for the door. I couldn't lose this opportunity.

"Excuse me." I pasted on an awe-filled smile and stepped to the side, blocking him. Waving a hand at his embroidery and hat, I showed him my phone with the other. "Would you mind terribly if I got a picture? I'm new to Tallahassee." My heart thudded in my chest as I waited for my ribs to shatter.

Instead, he beamed and shrugged. "I'd be obliged, Ma'am." He certainly spoke with a southwestern accent, but he was too pasty to have spent much time in the sun.

"What's going on, Kristen?" Marie asked with a tight tone.

Finn finished up their interview, saying good-bye.

I took two good shots, front and a slight angle. "Thank you so much. I'm Lacey."

His smile had the same cockiness as David's, as if knowing he had a strong jaw and chin, but he didn't offer a name. Instead, he tipped his hat in a classic western television show fashion. "Have a good day, Ma'am." Perhaps curvy and curly didn't warrant his name. He wasn't my type, either.

"Kristen?" Marie's voice rose.

The comms were silent. The noise in the room dimmed with each pounding of my pulse. I texted the pictures to Tomas, then lifted my phone to my ear, the one without the comms. "Hey, I just met a real-life cowboy."

"Get out, now." Marie spoke each word firmly.

"No, I didn't get his name. He was just finishing his lunch and left the deli I'm at." I smiled as the employee making sandwiches glanced at me.

"Kristen. I don't like this."

"I'm almost ready to order, but I'll call you back in a few minutes when I'm eating."

"Got them," Tomas said. "Running now. Good pictures."

"That was foolish. You've should have left immediately."

I didn't answer either of them, but left the dim-witted smile on my face as my heart pounded. The temptation to look behind me through the glass to the street hung heavy on my chest. I flexed my fingers, but the bones didn't break.

Behind me, the door opened and rang, causing me to jump. I glanced to the side, and caught a woman's hand holding a purse. I stared forward, glazed.

"What can I get you?" The woman ahead of me had finished ordering, and the server watched me with his eyebrows raised, expectant and perhaps frustrated at my glassy-eyed stare.

"Grilled cheese. Chips. Sweet tea." I'd planned to be more personable — perhaps get them to talk about Sally, but all I could think about was the cowboy. Maybe this was the piece we were missing all along.

I shuffled along as the line moved. Cowboy might be a regular at the deli, which could tie him to Sally, but he hadn't been on our witness list. He might just be a coincidence, but he tied in nicely if he was a customer at the deli.

That didn't eliminate Barry Weir as a suspect.

"Jacob Soros," Tomas said. I had to hope he'd be checking the register transactions to confirm. "Sending a preliminary report to email. I've got programs running to track his movements for the last few days."

If Jacob did pay with cash, he might have been here the day Sally died. I waited as the young man rang up my order.

"Nice job," David said, "wrangling the cowboy."

"Good work." Finn sounded frustrated. I could hear their footsteps on pavement. I hoped his tone had more to do with David, than me.

I didn't look out the front window until I pulled out my purse to pay. No villainous cowboy waited on the sidewalk to crumble my bones. If he had been our attacker, I hadn't risen to the level of enemy with him. I'd never considered trying to touch him to see if he were a dwarf or merfolk. There was still so much to learn. Had I been reckless with getting his photo?

David spoke loudly into the comms. "I should have got her number. You totally cramp my style." A door closed sharply in my comms, and I assumed they'd gotten back to their car.

"My *style* is this case." Finn *did* sound annoyed.

"Did you see those legs?"

I found a table and tuned out the comms. Cars and pedestrians passed the deli windows on their way to their business of the day. Two gruesome deaths had occurred this week, but they didn't slow down anyone.

The grilled cheese turned out pretty good, for not having a grill. I ate slowly, studying the incoming customers and waiting for an opportunity to speak with the manager.

David, rambling about his night with Lindsey, was cut off by Tomas. "Jacob Soros was in Panama City when the last two attacks occurred. I've confirmed receipts and even have him on a traffic cam at the hotel entrance."

I sagged with disappointment holding a chip in the air, fingers pausing before my mouth. Responding would be strange in the busy deli, and what did I have to say?

Perhaps it had been Barry Weir all along. It had been *my* searches that led to the name. I just couldn't feel a part of the team sitting in the deli while they were out risking their lives.

I finished my lunch, dumped my trash, and approached the counter, earning warning glances from those in line. I leaned over to peer in the back, but the manager hadn't shown the entire time.

Flashing an apologetic grimace, I asked, "Is the manager, Mr. Bebelle, here?"

The server's lips tightened, then he dashed to the back, and I heard muffled voices. When he returned, the manager followed on his heels.

He smiled with a bad imitation of friendliness. "Can I help you?"

I discretely showed him my badge. "Just a couple questions."

The false smile quickly soured. "I already spoke to you people. I don't have time."

Glancing at the customer at the register, I spoke quietly. "I know this is an inconvenient time, but I just need a discrete conversation. I don't want to make public any of the disturbance from the other day." I hated not saying Sally's name and reminding the little toad of the family that mourned her, but I didn't want to involve everyone in the conversation.

He fumed silently, then nodded toward the front door. "Outside. We can speak privately."

I had hoped he would invite me into the back office, but I nodded, then gestured for him to lead the way. "Thank you."

A number of customers, likely regulars who knew Mr. Bebelle, watched us leave, but no one said anything. He stalked to the curb. "What?"

"Do you know a Jacob Soros?" I wanted to gauge his reactions. There needed to be some connection to the deli, even if Jacob wasn't our suspect anymore.

He shook his head. "Don't know the name."

"Xavier Vasquez?"

"Yeah. Nice guy. Always a smile. Comes in once a week."

Unless he's shooting at you, I thought. "Barry Weir?"

The manager shrugged. "Nope."

"Emily Brown?"

He rolled his eyes. "Yes. She's in every day for a pastrami melt. Takes it to go, thank god."

"Is she difficult?"

"Fussy. Why do you care?" He snorted. "Is this a new crime that the government came up with? I've got a list for you starting with customers and ending with purveyors."

"When was she last here?"

"I saw her in line when I brought out quarters."

"Today?"

He frowned. "Yes. That's what I said."

Tomas swore in my comms. "She's not taking her phone with her."

"Has she been in every day this week?"

"I don't see everyone every day. I wouldn't know."

"Was she here when Sally Oswald died?"

"Probably, but I didn't see her. She comes every day. I told you that." He gestured to the deli. "I can't stand out here repeating everything you already know. This is lunch hour. We're busy."

He hadn't been out of the back the entire time I'd been there, but that didn't mean he wasn't working. "Okay. I'll check in if I have more questions." I needed to think about what our correction in Emily's activities meant.

Grumbling under his breath, the manager returned to the deli, leaving me on the sidewalk. I turned to study the crosswalk where Wendall had died during the first attack. He'd been swearing and cars had been honking. The business on the corner next to the deli storefront was an association of some sort, and they had never appeared busy. Across the street on the other corner, the restaurant only opened for dinner. I walked toward the end of the street.

Tomas's tone was calmer than his last response. "She pays by debit card, every day. There are no transactions the day Sally died."

So she hadn't come to the deli for her everyday meal. "Well, that seems odd, doesn't it?" I asked. Tomas didn't answer.

"What's odd?" asked Marie.

I reached the corner and walked with the light past the stains from Wendall's death. "Emily was not at the deli the day Sally died."

"We knew that."

I didn't explain, perhaps she hadn't heard the manager's comments over the other chatter. At the time, Finn had been talking with David and the comms were loud. I needed to mull this over.

The rain and cloud cover had left the temperature moderate, and I wanted to visit the other scenes. They were just down Park Avenue.

I listened to Finn and David's interview. The man hadn't seen the accident, only the slow down. I'd likely added his license with my video.

"I'm taking a walk down Park," I said. The street didn't appear very busy for being so close to city blocks. Most of the buildings in the area were residences.

Work on the porch had begun where George Dillon had plowed his car into the yard. The neighborhood approaching it had little noise. His loud music could have been disturbing, but there was almost no one nearby even at midday.

The park across the street had a lone man walking his dog. There was one house next to a lot with a few cars. I continued downhill, watching the two men working on the porch.

A few cars passed as I crossed the intersection. They sped to the bottom of the hill where I believed I spotted Beverly Court and the little office I'd stepped into. The next light would be where Ben Williams had gone through a red light, getting hit by the SUV. I'd go that far.

"Kristen, where are you now?" Marie asked.

"Heading down to Franklin and Park, where the last accident was."

"Why?" Her tone wasn't condemning, just curious.

I've got nothing better to do? "I wanted to walk Park Avenue; it's all been happening here."

"Okay. Keep me updated."

I had passed Beverly Court when Tomas popped onto the comms, pitch higher than normal. "I've got Barry

Weir. He turned on his phone again. He's on Tram Road heading toward Tallahassee. If he doesn't turn into Waterford, then we have eleven minutes before he hits 319 and other roads he can disappear on. Sending coordinates."

By his breathing, Finn jogged. "South of me?"

"Yes. Six or eight minutes."

My chest grew heavy. I hoped Barry was our culprit, mainly to end this. However, I worried about Finn, and I hated being excluded.

Tomas swore a short string of curses. "He turned his phone off again."

"Send locals from both ends to blockade. I hate to risk any officers. Finn, David, stop him." Marie spoke calmly, but I'd learned to hear the slight variations. She wanted this to end as much as we all did.

"Good luck," I said.

I considered calling a ride when I got to the intersection, then crossed on a whim. Sitting at the hotel didn't seem appealing. I'd rather be out and moving when Finn and David closed in on Barry, instead of sitting in a hotel room. Across Franklin Boulevard, a quiet neighborhood continued and Park Avenue rose slightly, curving out of sight. I was only a couple blocks from where Marie and David had been attacked.

Tomas's high pitch spiked at the start of his comment. "Seven minutes. Local's ETA is nine. I've diverted them to a position on Tram behind 319."

"Agreed," said Marie. "You're on your own, Finn."

"What am I? The lightning rod, oh yay." David made light of the situation, but he couldn't ignore the injuries he had just gone through.

I watched the cars and traffic lights from where I stood at the intersection. Finn and David were quiet, their car the only noise over the comms. "I'm going to see if Emily is home."

"Why?" Marie asked quickly. Was I interrupting the big chase?

I gestured to the south where all the excitement was happening. "She didn't show up for lunch the day Sally died. I'd like to know why."

"Be careful."

SEVENTEEN

The slope up Park Avenue had a lovely amount of shade, and the buildings on each side abandoned any sense of the city, turning instead to brick apartments and houses. The air still held its fresh rain scent, except when a truck roared past with oversized wheels and stacks spitting black smoke.

This section of Tallahassee had turned into a quiet residential neighborhood just a few blocks from the businesses surrounding the deli. I hadn't walked very far.

Tomas broke the silence on the comms. "Two minutes."

In the background, I heard Finn's engine slowing, preparing for their showdown with Barry Weir. "We're here past 319. There's some traffic. I'm only blocking eastbound, and leaving inbound to Tallahassee open."

David chuckled. "I'm going start jogging toward our little paranoid friend. Wish me luck."

His comment reminded me of our earlier conversation, and I couldn't help myself. "Break a leg."

"That's my girl." David sounded pleased.

I wondered what kind of expression Marie had. We might be close to the end of our case.

The hill had worked my legs, and I wondered at my folly. The top of the road was heavily wooded with a bridge over railroad tracks. I couldn't see them yet, but remembered passing over them. The apartments where Marie and David had been attacked were on the far side.

The comms went quiet, and I tried not to huff as I climbed. If Barry attacked David, I would turn and call for a ride. I shivered at the thought and hoped that Yan's Pin would protect Finn. The shade disappeared as I reached the bridge, and warmth pushed through the cloudy skies.

If Barry Weir were not our suspect, then I would be doing the right thing, following up leads. I wanted to be in the thick of it, but I was doing what I could.

"I think this is him." David sounded serious finally. "I'm keeping to the side of the road until he gets closer."

My pulse sped, even though I was nowhere near the action. The cool glade around the railroad tracks appeared incongruously calm compared to what David and Finn were attempting.

"Almost here. Keep on truckin', Buddy. How's he look to you, Finn?"

"I wouldn't have a sure shot at this distance." Finn's voice was tight.

I strode quicker across the top of the bridge, peering over to the back of the apartments and the parking lot where Marie and David had been attacked. A railing blocked the steep hill down, so I continued on the sidewalk along the side of the building.

"Okay. This is me pulling my weapon," said David. "I'm stepping out into the road. Please shoot him if I go down, Finn. I don't want to be run over in that condition."

Returning to the shade, I barely watched where I walked. The comms were my only focus.

"Hey, Buddy. This is me waving you down with my badge. Why did it have to rain? This asphalt is soaked." David snorted. "He's slowing down. Got him, Finn?"

"A pretty good shot. Reflection on the windshield, though."

"I'm still standing, so there's that."

Striding downhill, I passed the end of the railing. I almost continued ahead to the side street and to the front of the building. A worn path cut from the sidewalk into the grass, then curved around to the back side of the apartments.

"Barry Weir, Federal agent." David sounded almost officious. "Stop the car."

I immediately regretted my shortcut as the grass between the apartment and the road had soaked up a lot of rain, turning the ground to mud and hidden puddles.

"Look at me, standing and everything. Barry Weir, come out of the car."

"You can't just stop me and search the vehicle without cause." Barry sounded a little whiny over the comms.

"And yet, here I am, gun in hand, telling you to get out of the car. Searching it hadn't sounded interesting until you just mentioned it."

I slipped, dropping a knee into wet grass. Mud covered my shoes. I smiled, though, as David hadn't been attacked. Barry might not be our culprit.

"This is illegal. I'll sue. I'm recording this." Barry's tone had risen to indignant anger.

"C'mon, step out of the vehicle." David sighed. "Finn, I've got another car coming. I think it might be safe to come up here and direct traffic."

I relaxed as I reached the back corner of the building

at the edge of the parking lot and studied the familiar scene where we'd waited with David and Marie after the attack. The stains were visible from here. I thought the little Kuru were supposed to clean that up.

Emily's door waited for me, so I continued.

"Let's get that hoodie off," said David.

An engine started, and Finn spoke quietly. "Moving up to join David. I've got two vehicles closing in on Barry Weir's car."

I dallied in the heat, not wanting to be inside Emily's apartment if anything happened. One of the residents smoked outside the apartments, not noticing me.

"Okay, cell phone, in on your car seat." David's voice shifted and I heard light pats, as if he searched Barry. "Alright, what's in this pocket?"

"You have no right. No cause. I'm going to sue you and your mother." Barry had reached anger, and still David was standing.

"That's going to be tricky. Ooh, what's this?" Plastic crackled in the comms. "Crap, this smells good. I'm going to have to confiscate this."

"It's medicinal."

"I'm not that picky. Besides, some of that stuff is decent."

I could be fairly confident that Barry didn't have the ability to break bones. Perhaps he'd left the crystal some-where. Part of me had hoped we'd closed the case by apprehending him, but the other part still wanted to be in on the take down. It was selfish, really. I didn't think Emily would be a great help, but I couldn't think of anyone else they'd let me talk to. Why hadn't she had her daily lunch the day Sally had died?

The smoker had finally spotted me standing in a parking spot and staring blankly.

Over the comms, Finn's engine turned off in the background, then his door closed. I didn't think there was much more to worry about with Barry Weir.

"Pyre, I think we're going to want transport for our friend." David coughed lightly. "This car is packed with crap we'll need to go through."

"Got it," said Tomas.

I started up the sidewalk. "Well, I'm going to Emily's now. I'll go off comms, if you don't mind. I'd like to know why she didn't continue her daily diner routine. She might simply have been too depressed, with Xavier added to her other problems."

"Comms stay on," Marie said.

Now that they were safe, I didn't see the point in listening to their conversations with Barry, not when I couldn't pay attention. "Okay." I left the comms active and strode toward the apartment door.

Emily's dead orchids still hung in their hangers, but the bright ceramic frog looked shinier from the rain. I didn't hear anything from inside. She might not even be home. Kicking as much mud as I could from my shoes, I knocked once on her door before Tomas interrupted me.

He sounded tense, his voice a little higher pitch than usual. "Kristen, where are you?"

I knocked two more times on Emily's door. "Emily's."

"Can you leave?" he asked.

"Why?" I heard a thump and movement inside.

Tomas cleared his throat. "Emily *was* at the diner the day Sally died. Her card was declined. Sally died as she rang up the next customer. I should have found this."

Emily opened the door, her face turning sour. She wore her threadbare robe, a faded T-shirt, and black yoga pants. Her eyes were red from crying. "What do *you* want?"

My throat knotted with a fist-sized lump, but I smiled

and swallowed it down. "I'm not really here on FBI business, I just wanted to see if you were okay." I could just listen for a second, then retreat out of the apartment complex.

Marie spoke quietly. "Get out of there, Kristen." Marie would have a plan for something like this. It might involve Emily's death.

A chill rose up my neck. "If you're busy, I apologize. I just knew you'd been through so much. I should have just called." If I left, walking with all my bones intact, then perhaps Marie would let Finn try to sweet talk his way in, wearing Yan's Pin.

Emily's expression softened. "That's very kind. But you have a dog as well, so you know."

"Yes," I lied. "I just wanted to make sure you were okay." Another smile and I could turn and walk away. I almost mentioned Xavier, and stopped myself. Emily likely pined for him. I didn't need her angry. "I'll let you be."

"Come in. I'll make us sweet tea." Emily stepped back. "I could use some company."

"Don't." Marie's voice was an order, not just the word.

"I didn't mean to intrude. I'll just . . ." I gestured weakly at the parking lot.

Emily's expression darkened. "I thought you liked the tea?"

"Loved it. So did Finn. We'll come back and . . ."

"What game are you playing?" Emily frowned.

"Get out of there." Marie had never sounded this concerned. Each word.

"No game." My chest pounded and I swayed. My smile trembled slightly. I stepped over the threshold. "I didn't want to intrude."

Tomas swore when the door closed behind me.

"Night storms. Finn, get there now. David, stow it. I want to be able to hear."

My pulse raced as I stepped into Emily's incense-scented apartment. The tissues still dominated the coffee table, but the peanut butter cookies had been replaced with chocolate chip. An empty coaster sat among the wads of paper. The remote rested on the edge of the couch. The keyboard and seat had been neatly restored after David's musical performance.

Emily waved at the beige couch. "Sit, sit. I'll get the tea."

I swallowed and fought a shiver as I touched her shoulder. "I'll help." No traces of the Mer realm hinted at an illusion. We could be overreacting, as we had with Xavier and Barry.

Walking behind her, I hoped she wouldn't see the mud I'd tracked in. Killed over dirty shoes had never been a worry before. "You've been okay?" I asked. What did you ask someone who's been out of work, lost their dog, and had their friend arrested?

"It never ends." She pulled two glasses off a drying rack, placing them in front of a container of powdered iced tea. "They held my last check for an extra day, no word about that ahead of time. My electric went through, but my cable payment bounced with my card overdrawn. It took half a day to fix, moving money from savings, and still no television."

"I'm sorry they did that." I leaned against the counter, trying to appear relaxed as I studied her. She wore a worn navy-blue T-shirt which draped past her hips so long that I couldn't tell if her yoga pants had pockets.

I didn't notice any bulges on the right side of her robe.

She dumped two spoonfuls of brown powder into a glass and handed it to me, motioning toward the fridge.

"Dale loaned me some money. He's had good luck. Filled up his U-Haul."

I poured cold water into the glass, moistening the top layer and leaving dried dust at the base. She offered the second glass to me, and I swapped with her. "You're so lucky to have him."

"I suppose." Emily shrugged as she stirred the one glass.

I stirred the tea in the second glass holding my position. When we returned to the living room I hoped to see the left pocket of her robe.

No. I didn't have to find the crystal, just get out of the apartment with my bones intact. David and Finn could handle the rest. Maybe we could break in while she slept. How close to her did the crystal need to be?

"Finn and David are ten minutes out," Tomas said over the comms.

"Get out of there, Kristen. Gulp the tea and make an excuse." Marie spoke in a tight, low whisper.

The clinking stopped, and I turned up to find Emily waiting for me with an odd expression, the spoon placed on the counter, and her hand pointed toward the living room. How long had I been staring at her robe? A chill rose up my neck. "Thank you." I lifted the glass.

She spoke behind me in a surly tone. "You seem preoccupied."

I didn't turn as I approached the couch. "Sorry. We're still working on the case. Occupational hazard — meandering thoughts."

"I figured you actually came to interrogate me some more." Suspicion and annoyance hung in her tone.

My heart froze, but I forced a smile. "Not at all. You told us everything. Very helpful, too. We found the man in the cowboy hat, thanks to your description." I sat at the left end of the couch, so I could see her other pocket if she sat beside me.

Emily looked surprised as she walked around the coffee table. "Did he have anything to do with that man's death? I still don't really understand what you are investigating." Her tone had calmed, becoming casual again.

I sipped my tea slowly, staring at the couch, waiting for the moment she sat. Fuzzy blue cloth folded, then as she pressed into the cushion, the pocket sagged with weight. My chest tightened. "We'll be talking to him soon to see if he saw anything. We still are trying to find answers."

My answer waited an arm's length away. She drank her tea, glancing at the blank television. I should get out and let Finn deal with the crystal. What if Yan's Pin didn't work as they expected? She'd fold David like origami. I drank half of the cold tea and placed it on the coaster.

Emily studied me. "Could it be a toxin? I heard one of the girls at the deli took sick too."

"That's certainly a possibility." I took a deep breath after I lied.

With my left hand beside my thigh, I pinched into the soft Mer realm and formed a lifting spell. A blue-green stream wound around my back and slid down beige cushions to creep over to Emily's robe. Poking a thin tendril inside, I reached for the crystal.

"Hmm?" She rubbed at her side, almost touching my spell before I dissolved it.

Heart pounding, I took up my glass and sipped again. "The tea really is good."

I was being foolish. However, we all took risks. There was no guarantee my teammates would survive. Finn had a husband. it was time for me to step up. Somehow, the decision calmed me slightly.

"When I was working full-time, I could afford my

favorite. Little bottles which came in a four-pack. Expensive." Emily tilted her head, staring at her drink and swirling it around. The edges of her mouth twitched as if she might frown — something I really didn't want her doing at the moment.

Happy thoughts. My tongue felt like sandpaper when I tried to swallow. I put down my glass and began forming two lifting spells with my left hand. What I planned was no different than pranks I'd played at school. Almost no one had ever suspected me. Of course, my bones wouldn't have crumbled if they had.

"Well, I'm sure you'll be back to work soon." I leaned in, resting my right elbow on my thigh, and smiled encouragingly.

I formed the third lifting spell with my right hand. Holding my breath, I sent the stream of Mer low past her shins arcing back up to the remote.

Emily rocked her head back and forth lightly, as if weighing my comment. If she moved about too much, she'd feel my spells. "I'm beginning to feel old and used up."

The two spells from my left hand I laced over my back, blue tendrils poised at her pocket. I watched it all from my peripheral vision keeping my eyes locked on her face.

I toppled the remote to the floor with a thud, leaving the spell active, but unattached.

"Bother." Emily started to place her drink down, seemed to realize I had used her only coaster available, and with her left hand, held her glass up over the table as she reached down with her right hand to retrieve the remote. She grunted and her robe shifted with the movement.

The first of my two spells slid open her pocket smoothly. I pulled it wide enough that the weight of the crystal pulled off her hip. My second tendril dove in and started wrapping until I sensed it grasp firmly. I released the distracting spell from my right hand.

The television remote in her fingers, Emily rose back up. "Ungh." Her grunt startled me.

I yanked the crystal out so quickly, I worried it might fly over the couch. My heart raced, and I thought she'd surely see it pulsing in my neck. Double wrapping Mahakala's quartz in two spells, I retracted them over my shoulders.

When I took in a breath, it became a sharp inhale that Emily noticed. She peered at my wide eyes.

The crystal lay in my left palm. My ears pounded with my pulse. I had no enemies. That left no one that the artifact would need to hurt.

"What is it?" Emily asked.

I reached for the remains of my tea with my right hand, pocketing the crystal with my left into my jacket. "I realized I need to call my boarder. They hadn't expected me to be gone this long."

My knees wobbled as I stood. At what point did Mahakala's quartz stop serving one person and transfer to another? I had no intention of annoying Emily and finding out. "Thank you so much for the tea. I'm sorry you've gone through so much over the past couple of weeks. I'll call before I come barging over again."

"Finally," Marie said over the comms. "Get out of there." She would be pissed when I told her what I'd done.

Emily shrugged, put the remote back on the cushion, and stood. "I appreciate the visit. People are so self-centered and false." She shifted her tea to her right hand and wiped her left toward her pocket.

Panic rising, I shoved my glass at her, occupying her free hand.

False, like me. "Thank you, again." With no idea how

she'd behave after she found the crystal missing, nor how Mahakala's quartz would react, I nearly sprang for the door.

A few steps, and I'd know if I'd survived. I didn't wait for her. My hand shook as I fumbled the knob. My jaw clenched as it turned and daylight hit my eyes. It didn't seem nearly as gloomy as it had before; in fact, even the clouds shone like freedom.

EIGHTEEN

y legs trembled as I closed the door. "I'm out. I've got the quartz."

The earthy scent of growth hung in the air as I tottered down the sidewalk. I would have run but for the older man walking into the courtyard with bags of groceries dangling from his fingertips. Each step I took seemed like a grace as I gained distance between me and Emily.

"How?" Marie demanded. "Report." She did not use her happy voice, if she had one.

"I used my abilities." I nodded to the elderly man as we passed. "She didn't know." Shakily, I put my hand in my coat jacket and touched the crystal. It was warm, and solid, and beckoning. "I pulled it from her robe. I hope she just thinks it dropped out or something." The quartz had range limitations to attack. I quickened my pace as I reached the asphalt and nearly jogged for the exit of the parking lot.

"Don't touch it."

I shivered and pulled my hand out of my pocket. "Too

late." I'd been holding it, and the release of it felt like a loss. I wanted to press my fingers against its solid surface again. "Why?"

"Some objects have a lure to them. They want to be used."

Considering Emily, that made sense. Troubled, especially with all she'd gone through, she considered mere drivers to be an enemy. Perhaps the world appeared arrayed against her, and the slightest aggravation aligned her focus. I had no animosity toward anyone, at the moment. A dread rose in me, and I tried not to imagine I carried a live bomb in my jacket pocket.

I took a deep breath. The quartz should be safe with me. "Do we get it to the vault now?"

"That's the plan. Finn will pick you up." Marie's voice was calm, but they had to consider me a danger.

I stopped at the sidewalk, slowed to a walk along the front of the apartments, and headed for Park Avenue and some shade. Staring up into the green canopy, I let my heart settle. We — I'd closed the case with no more deaths. Emily Brown could not be held responsible, I assumed, since she hadn't even known what she was doing. I wanted to believe she would have given up the crystal, but we hadn't taken that chance. As my fear dwindled, pride in my accomplishment rose, not without some chagrin on my part.

I barely noticed when Finn pulled down the side street, peering at me and smiling. If he considered me a threat, he didn't show it. "Pyre is pissed. Get in." David wasn't in the car.

"Stow it, Finn." Marie, however, did not sound pleased over the comms.

"Sorry." I jogged across the street and around the front to sit in the passenger seat. "Where's David?" I hadn't heard him get out, or them even talking over the comms.

"Getting our stuff from the hotel. He'll meet us at the airport." Finn's grin and tone made me smile. "I want to hear everything, but first, glove box."

He took off slowly down the side street, letting me open the compartment before buckling. On top of some papers was a cast iron box the size of my fist. "For the crystal?" I asked.

"Yep. Should negate some of its effect."

The plain, utilitarian box had been well built with hinges at the back and a secure clasp which I had to pry open. Pulling a stream of Mer realm, I pulled open my jacket pocket carefully and sent the tendril in. The firm sensation of the crystal reacted to my spell, and I wound it carefully. I didn't want to drop it under the seat.

I had barely glimpsed Mahakala's quartz when I'd stolen it. The size of my thumb, it could have been any crystal were it not for the beige shape inside. I paused, studying it. The object had been inscribed with possibly Akkadian sigils on every bit of the surface. "Is that bone?"

"Possibly. We'll leave it for the Kuru to document, then it disappears into the vault."

I dropped the crystal into the iron box. "Glove box?"

"Keep it in your pocket for now. Go bag when we get to the plane. Buckle up." Finn cleared his throat. "How did you get it off her?"

"Three lifting spells." I shoved the box in my jacket and reached for the seatbelt. "One to drop something and distract her. A second to pull open her pocket. The last to reach in and grab it. When she told me Sally had been the one to decline her card, I figured she had to be carrying Mahakala's quartz. I only guessed that it was in her robe pocket."

Finn frowned. "Three spells simultaneously with that kind of precision. Where did you learn that?"

I shrugged. "I've always been good with the Mer realm."

He chuckled. "*Good* doesn't exactly give your ability justice."

NINETEEN

The box traveled back to Atlanta in my go bag. When we arrived at the office, Finn accompanied me to the archives. Luggage draped off us as he left David to the office and opened the door to a room beside our employee lounge. Long and narrow, it had white drawers on all the walls except the entrance. Each had numbers like security deposit boxes. A thin steel table ran fifteen feet down the center.

"Anywhere on the table," Finn said. He leaned against the wall beside the door. "I can't wait to get home and shower."

My stomach tensed as I unzipped my backpack to retrieve the iron box. I hated leaving the crystal in the room; it felt unprotected. Could the Kuru be trusted? After all we'd gone through to get it, I wanted it safe — with me.

I shivered and hurriedly put it on the table with a loud clank. Swallowing, I focused on zipping up my pack.

"You okay?" Finn studied me.

My lips moved, but I didn't say what I wanted; I wanted to keep the crystal. "Yeah, fine. Hungry."

Marie had insisted that we keep the comms on until we dropped off the box. I still startled when she spoke. "Pack it up for the night. Good job." There hadn't been a word from her the entire flight. "Take the morning off tomorrow. Come in after lunch for full reports."

"Got it, Pyre." Finn took his comms out of his ear.

I turned mine off and did the same. If she held a resentment over my behavior, I'd rather get the reprimand over and done with. I knew she would have rather I'd just left and had Finn take care of Emily. "Is that normal? Shouldn't we focus on reports now?"

"Tomas will have preliminaries ready for Stacey and — everyone." We stepped into the hall. He motioned me toward the armory to stow our ammunition and his gun. "Tomas's reports are usually better than ours. We'll still have to file them."

"What will happen to Barry?" I asked.

"He's been released."

We exited into the hall, and he kept his go bag with him on the way to the elevator. Full of laundry and missing half my snacks, I slipped mine over my shoulder and followed him.

"Did the team mute my comms when I had the crystal?"

He punched the button for the first floor and nodded. "We had to assess the situation."

I didn't respond. We walked silently down the halls until we exited the building. He stopped at the edge of the parking lot. "You did good. Pyre will let you know you went off protocol, but I understand the situation. Take the break. Get some rest. It'll be fine."

On the ride home, I squelched the feeling of loss and the image of the iron box alone on the steel table. Whatever magic drove me toward the crystal would have to eventually fade.

Behind me, the sun would be setting in the next hour or so, and the late traffic made the drive a little slower. With a later start at the office tomorrow, I could get in some exercise in the morning. Right now, a shower sounded good.

The apartment held some heat from the day and smelled stuffy, so I slid the backpack onto the counter with my magic and headed into the bedroom to open a window. A door closed out front, then someone knocked on my mine.

Astrid had on a light blue T-shirt and jean shorts. "Hey, sorry to bother you." She held a small box, and I recognized my mail immediately.

"I'd forgotten about my soft pastels. Come in." I took the box and inspected it. It didn't appear too beaten up. Shipping was a horror on delicate supplies.

She stepped in, noting the backpack. "You were on a trip." Tucking a strand of blue hair behind her ear, she pursed her lips. "Work. I'll let you rest."

I wanted a shower, but wasn't sure I could sleep. "I'm making tortellini. Alfredo sauce. Have you eaten?"

Astrid smiled. "I have. Maybe tomorrow night?"

I had no idea how late I'd be doing reports. "I don't go into the office until late. I have no idea of my schedule."

She brightened. "Breakfast then. There is a restaurant I have been wanting to try, and you have a car."

I nodded. "Thank you for getting my package. Breakfast sounds great. I want to get some time at the gym first. I'll check in with you when I get back."

Astrid grinned. "Perfect. See you then."

After Astrid left, I headed to the bedroom to strip off clothes for a shower in *my* bathroom. Later, when I made dinner, I'd call Jade. She would still be worrying about her vision.

The shower sputtered as I turned it on. I might even make the tortellini. Tomorrow already sounded pleasurable, except for the part about standing in front of Marie and having her chastise me.

In only a couple minutes, I stood under steaming water and finally began to relax.

The next day when I arrived at the office, Finn was already sitting at his desk. He worked at his computer, likely filling out his report. He glanced up and winked. I dropped my go bag in the cabinet and purse in my drawer, then approached him. I leaned down and whispered, "Should I go in?" I pointed to Marie's office.

His braids swayed as he shook his head. "She'll call you in. Haven't seen her myself."

I grimaced and skittered back to my desk. In my email, Tomas had sent high resolution pictures of Mahakala's quartz. The urge to retrieve it returned, but less intensely than it had been yesterday. The Kuru took excellent photographs. Tomas had even separated the inscriptions from the photographs into a detailed square which appeared so exact that it could have been peeled off the bone.

The designs were Akkadian, but of no configuration I'd ever seen. Not even close.

My report was done in an hour, and David showed up shortly after that. He replied to my raised eyebrow, "What am I supposed to report on? Dr. Southwark's breath? The convalescence facilities in the weight room?"

"I think you'd be good at a dead lift."

He snorted and pointed at me as he passed. "Stop making fun of the wounded."

"Not what I in tendoned."

"That was horrible." David chuckled and sat down behind me.

It took another hour before Marie called me into her office. I never heard her door open. Behind me, she spoke from the doorway. "Kristen?"

Startled, I jumped up, nearly knocking over my cold tea. "Yes."

She watched me, appearing as healthy as she ever had been. Her bald head and face had no visible bruises, and her eyes were bright and focused. Her expression was unreadable.

My stomach knotted as I hurried toward her. She turned and walked to her desk. Assuming, I closed the door behind me. "Sorry," I said.

She sat down, motioning me to the red and gold sofa. She waited until I turned at the couch. "You did good." Tiberius, her orange tabby, rubbed up against her legs.

My eyes widened, and my eyebrows arched. "I thought you'd be upset." I perched on the edge of the cushions.

"Concerned. I don't tell you to do something because I want to be in control. I need my people as safe as they can be. Our work is dangerous and often fatal. I survive, and those who work with me often die. Few retire." Her lips pursed. "I'd rather you all were in the latter group. You'll learn when to take the initiative, or not." She waved her hand. "Your magic worked. You survived. You didn't directly disregard an order, and I understand the delicate circumstances you were in. How you ended up finding Mahakala's quartz I don't understand, but you have that knack, don't you?" She cocked her head and leaned down to stroke Tiberius.

I shrugged. "I think I just couldn't sit at the hotel anymore."

She snorted and appeared sympathetic, but she'd been

out of commission trying to heal. "What did you find out about the rave massacre?"

The quick change in subject startled me. This was hardly the reprimand I'd expected. "Nothing. I've got more questions, mainly. Were they all from the same economic class? A status where they might not be noticed missing? How did they find out about the party? Were they all invited?"

She leaned forward, eyebrows furrowed. "Invited?"

"Joe Capra and Michael Compton were given invitations."

"By whom?"

"A girl. He didn't know her. Dark hair, dark eyes."

For a long moment, her eyes held mine, then she nodded. "Keep at it." She gestured toward the door. "Grab Finn and get Mahakala's crystal in the Vault. Then meet us for dinner. Usual place."

I stood, unsure. I'd expected to be reamed for taking the crystal instead of waiting for Finn. "Are you healed now?"

"Fully? No." Marie smiled. "But I'd like a beer. Move it."

David smiled handsomely as I stepped out, as if he knew of my surprise at Marie's reaction. I ignored him and spoke to Finn. "She wants us to put it in the Vault, then head out for dinner."

Finn rose silently and only spoke when we exited into the hall. "All good?"

"I think so."

He opened the door to the archives, and the box sat on the table where I'd left it. Finn texted on his phone while I retrieved it. "Gary can make it."

It felt awkward to have the crystal back in my possession. I needed to not focus on it. "Is he happy to have you home?"

Finn moved to the armory door. "Yes, but he knew we'd been through something rougher than usual. I'd been short on the phone a couple nights."

I led the way inside and stared at the wooden door leading to the mysterious hall and the dragon-shifter, the Keeper. "Anthony always knew when I had a rough case. My ex."

He pulled out Yan's Pin and held it up. "If Gary had any idea, he still wouldn't be talking to me."

After knocking three times, Finn placed his hand against the wood. The closet had filled with the gray mist, and in that moment I thought of Jade. *Gray, like Tarus.* "I'm not in any danger here, am I?"

Finn frowned. "No. Why do you ask?"

As he disappeared into the mist, I followed him in. I hesitated as I closed the door. His silhouette formed in the glow of the tunnel ahead. I stepped beside him, torn between tossing the box into the tunnel and opening the door to leave. I forced myself to be calm and thought of the weather and seasons. My grandmother and mother would be digging out the winter leavings for the spring planting. Some of the perennials would already have green sprouting. The heady scent of herbs would drift up as we dug. There was no reason to panic.

As the hooded figure reached us, Finn did not automatically hand over the talisman. "Welcome, Keeper."

"Welcome, Finn."

I followed with the same courtesies, wanting to shove the box at the dragon-shifter.

Finn held out his talisman. "I return Yan's Pin."

Two long fingers pinched onto the tiny object. "I take Yan's Pin to my care."

I pushed the box forward, but Finn shook his head. "Remove it from the metal." He lowered his voice to a near whisper. "I bring Mahakala's quartz."

As ritualistic as they'd been, I should have known it wouldn't be just a dump and run. I unlatched the lid and opened it. Loathe to touch it again and tempt myself, I reached for the Mer realm.

It wasn't there. Realms were always — everywhere. A faint panic rose at its absence. My fingers flitted in the emptiness.

"No magic in here. You'll be okay." Finn nudged his chin toward the box.

Clearing my throat, I touched the welcoming, warm, smooth surface and hesitated, then stretched my arm out. "I bring Mahakala's quartz." My voice croaked, throat dry.

The Keeper bowed slightly. "I take Mahakala's quartz to my care." In a slow move, cold rough skin plucked the crystal from my fingers.

When we finished and had closed the wooden door behind me, I trembled as I reached for Mer and dug fingers into it. Ripples of blue rolled from my hand. "What happened?" I released the realm.

"I should have warned you. The Mer realm is not inside the vault. I have read that Haven and Dur-Alf exist there, and it is believed Salmhalla, but not the others. I'm not sure how David survived in there, but it's possible." He shrugged, his palms rising in the air. "We're safe now. The talisman is gone."

We were safe. *Safer.* I would describe what I could about the vault's mist to Jade, and see if that satisfied her fears. Her visions were something to consider. I didn't dismiss them, and the next time I was near Tarus, I'd be especially careful. My present concern was calming her fears. She felt responsible when she had a vision. In her present state, we could barely keep a conversation going for a couple minutes.

We gathered at the restaurant with outdoor seating beside the little airport the team used. Whenever we landed, I could spot the building and deck and there was always a lively crowd at midday and for dinner.

Outside, Marie sat alone at the table, her shining bald head a beacon in the sunlight. She already had her beer in hand — Loblolly, a double IPA from a local Georgia brewery. I'd been slowly trying their selections.

One of the regular servers spotted us heading toward her and nodded as he delivered a tray of drinks. Finn would get a cold brew or just plain water; he didn't drink. I hadn't decided on anything. The afternoon had been tense, then everything had worked out. The table had been set for five with waters, napkin rolls, and appetizer plates.

Marie peered at us. "Gary?"

Finn grinned and pointed toward the building. His husband couldn't have been more different than him with pale skin, a beard, and a solid paunch. However, his smile when he saw us blossomed as widely as Finn's.

I gave Gary a hug before Finn could grab him. "So what did you have to put in the fridge?" I asked quietly.

"Asparagus and Gruyère quiche. Fingerling potatoes," he whispered in my ear. Working from home, he tended to do the cooking and planned well ahead. He often ended up with leftovers when Marie decided she wanted a team dinner.

Finn pushed me aside jokingly to grab a kiss from Gary. I sat beside Marie.

David had intercepted our server. From his rapid questions, he was likely interrogating the man on the available wine selection.

Gary slid down beside Marie and kissed her cheek.

"Lovely as always, Marie. Glad everyone made it back in one piece." He glanced over his shoulder at David. "They did, didn't they?"

Lifting her beer, she cocked her head and peered at me. "Thanks to Kristen, all in one piece."

Tugging at his beard, Gary leaned against Finn. "Brought him home safe for me? You're my new favorite." He grabbed the water he rarely drank and offered a toast. Marie joined with her beer.

I blushed, wishing I had a drink. Boasting with the other detectives was never comfortable for me. A case needed to be solved; people had to be protected. "We're a team. I just got lucky."

Finn picked up his water. "Here's to luck, disguised as skill and intuition." His grin slid up on one side.

"Wait, wait." David jogged over, server chasing behind. "You can't toast me if I'm not here." He looked around the table and grimaced. "And certainly not with water. Wait for the wine."

"Stow it, David. Raise a glass for Kristen's success."

He rolled his eyes, took up the glass with two fingers, and winked at me. "To Kristen."

Red-faced, I grabbed my glass and took a sip with them. "Thank you." Now we could move on. People at a nearby table were watching us, drawn by David's theatrics, and perhaps his perfect form.

David mimicked a gag and handed the water to the server. "I'm assuming you'll celebrate with cheap ale?"

I picked up the menu. "I'm not sure. Let's play it by beer."

<<<<>>>>

AFTERWORD

A quick thanks and a hope that you enjoyed this story, if you did then a review is always helpful.

Would you be interested in a free short from David's perspective? An incident in his past?

If you haven't read it already, you can download from BookFunnel a very quick read. It'll sign you up for a mailing list during the download, but it won't activate unless you confirm on the follow up email.

David's Journal #21 https://BookHip.com/FRQGMPM

Demon

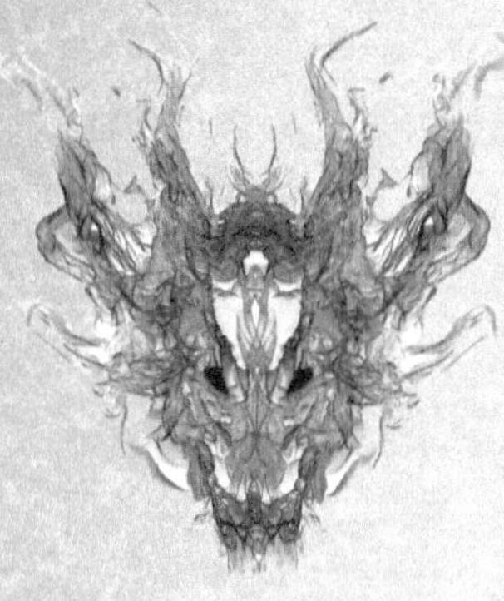

A demon is a rare inhabitant of the Tarus Realm who can be summoned to the Earth realm or cross of its own intent if given an opening. [1]

Their summoned forms often are a nightmarish mirror of their summoner with features designed to terrorize, such as claws, fangs, and horns. [1][2] Highly intelligent, they feed on strong emotions such as panic or rage. [2][3]

They are reported to rely on physical attributes for attack, but have been known to compel humans to act out their violence. [2][3]

(Cont. next page; Accounts of Demons in Tarus)

[1] Read Tinkanchtners's *The Art of Demonic Summoning*

[2] Read Kizurra's *Referene on Tarus Cryptids* Page 26 to 47

[2] Read Carey's *Of Demons and Jinns*

Dragon-shifter

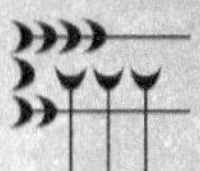

  The portion of a dragon exposed in the Earth realm which can mimic the aspect of a human.

  Most of what is known about dragon-shifters has come from archaic grimoires with questionable translations. [1][2] There is at least one resident on Earth to coordinate with the Consociation. [3] Reportedly, a dragon-shifter is an exact replica of a human, unless they intend otherwise. [2][4] A witch would know on contact.

  The details of their craft ability are shrouded in myth due to their self-expulsion from the Earth realm prior to the Akkadian wars was preceded by a slow withdrawal during the prior era. [1][2][4] They openly apologize for their interference with man, resulting in the rituals that brought about the vampires and werewolves. [3][5]

(Cont. next page; Role in Consociation)

[1] Read Yin's Volume IV of Realm Studies Pages 1340 to 1489

[2] Read Wooley's Anectdotal Studies of Salmhalla

[3] Read Ferno's Presentation of the Consociation

[4] Read Inhai Du Anya's Scriptures of the High Dragons Page 1-72

[5] Read Sover's On Madness

Draugr / Draughr

A common inhabitant of Tarus who can be summoned to the Earth realm, or cross of its own intent if given an opening. Territorial they tend toward an unusual compunction to protect valuables.

Tall and strong they present as humanoid on Earth with no skin and sharp black nails. They possess reflexes and speed beyond humans.[1] Savage and instinctual on a physical level. Relatively low intelligence.

Magical or Arcane abilities: None

Note the Akkadian ritual listed in the 1911 appendix

[1]Read Macrin's Journal for an in-depth biological reference compilation of Merfolk research of the Draugr

Dwarf / Dwarves

    Humanoid residents of Dur-Alf with a proclivity for exploration and research. Their earliest interactions with humans caused a wider disturbance than expected and their own sanctions for crossing to Earth were ignored by many of their more independant scholars and explorers. Brief conflicts existed between individuals as witches developed the ability to pass into the Dur-Alf realm.

Small in mass and stature, their biology is similar to Earth mammals. [1]

Conflicts erupted between humans and dwarves [2] as human witches and arcane users began to cross realms. Dwarves are especially biased against vampires.

(Cont. next page; Magical and Arcane usage)

[1] Read Macrin's Understanding Dwarven Physiology and Psyche

[2] Read Thant's War on Human Mutation

Kuru Kuru 

Mammallian bipedal residents of Dur-Alf though the only known description of their physical resemblance comes from two sources and both differ slightly. [1][2]

The Dwarves do acknowledge their presence and the Kuru Kuru have been given access to the Consociation. [3] They speak only to the Dragon delegation there and have some relationship with Dragons. [4]

Small in mass and stature, their biology is similar to Earth mammals with a flattened muzzle. Reports differ on fur (pictured), or with feathers. [1][2][3]

(Cont. next page; Magical suppositions)

[1] Read Kainin's Guide to Dur-Alf, Eden of the Realms

[2] Read Emily Randolp's Memoirs Among the Sprites

[3] Read Daesalu's Biography of Talat

[4] Read Ono Seyo's Conspiracy of the Consociation

Merfolk / Mer

Mer, called Merfolk by the Consociation, have the ability to transform into similar mammalian shapes upon interrealm movement. [1]

Little is known about their unaltered form except that it is a sea mammal of some type, hypothesized to be porpoise-like. [2]

Their longstanding habitation of Earth's oceans ceased at the point when Earth witches and arcane users began using the Mer realm in magic which coincided with the interrealm movement of humans to Dur-Alf. [3] Merfolk returned to Earth during the formation of the Consociation at the urging of the dwarves with whom they had long enjoyed diplomacy and trade. [4]

Many Mer research and work on Earth as part of their proposal to the Consociation for admittance. [5]

(Cont. next page; the impact of Merfolk on magical use by witches and the arcane)

[1] Read Sienna's Treatise on Earth's Devastation

[2] Read Tino Vangian Biography of Venis: Traitor of Mer

[3] Read Sienna's Treatise on Mer Isolation

[4] Read Tino Vangian Biography of Venis: Traitor of Mer

[5] Read Tino Vangian's Biograpy of Sienna

Revenant

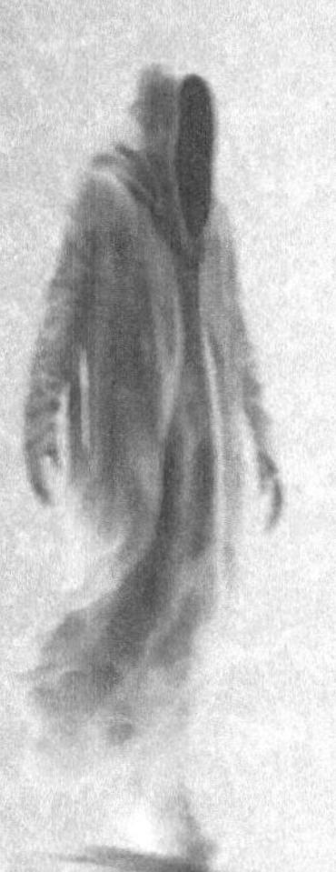

An inhabitant of Tarus which can be summoned to the Earth realm, or cross of its own intent if given an opening.

Disembodied in the Earth realm, they will seek to possess a humanoid corpse, or living entities with a weakened consciousness such as comotose or those near death.

Their corporeal control depends greatly on their prior experience.[1]

They range in intelligence and will avoid confrontation where possible.

Expellation is relatively simple depending on the skill of the witch.[2] Vampires have an innate ability to remove Revenants from their possessed hosts.

Magical or Arcane abilities: None

[1]Read Rasputin's Walks Among the Undead for a detailed observance of summoned Revenants

[2]See Appendix from 1892 - reference Possession

Vampire

A vampire is a human-born crossover to the Tarus realm. They are infected with a Tarus symbiotic life form initially misunderstood as a form of magic inherited from Tarus. [1] The infection can be summoned, gained through prolonged contact with Tarus, or transferred by blood-to-blood transfer with a vampire. [2]

The human cells are mutated to a far more resilient state and can be controlled to an extent which allows the vampire to change facial features and extend their life. [1] [3] Strength and speed are are increased with minimal muscular and bone alterations. [4] Vampires are entirely resistant to infection, disease, and toxins. [3] Mental acuity does not change. Emotional reactions remain, though extended life spans have brought interesting results. [1] [3] [4] [5]

(Cont. next page; the Tarus symbiote)

[1] Read Tonsun's *Illuminating the Mystery*

[2] Read William Beckett's *Becoming a Legend*

[3] Read Annan's *Study on Mutation*

[4] Read Anonymous *Confessions of Self-Hatred*

[5] Read Macrin's *Sapien Emotive Reponses* Pages 21-88

Werewolf / Dreamer / Hunter

Born human they have developed a psychic and realm connection to Ya Keya. They are affected by their interactions and develop biological alterations. The connection can be summoned, by a ritual interaction with the bodily fluids of a mature werewolf, or through intense submersion in Ya Keya.[1] Longevity varies [2]

Transmuted form:
They gain 15-20% more mass directly from the Ya Keya realm. Reflexes, strength, and speed increase by 10-30% beyond their human norms. Eyesight and hearing are more acute though more age dependant than other attributes.[2]

(Cont. next page; loss of Magic and Arcane usage)

[1] Read Kizurra's History of Akkadian Werewolves - the Dawn

[2] Read Demot's Monograph for an in-depth biological reference

Dur-Alf

Visible indications are a dark-green color and a crumbling or dusty consistency.

Dur-Alf is a planet realm similar to Earth in that it orbits a singular star; it is the fourth of eight known bodies in the system and does not have any satellites. There are major land-locked bodies of water and large polar ice caps. [1] Rivers and lakes abound in most regions except near equatorial deserts. The seasons are mild, and wildlife is plentiful. [1] [2] The only known transplants from Earth are kestrels and a variety of water birds including swans, geese, ducks, and kingfishers. [1] [2] [3]

Humans are no longer welcome or tolerated in the Dur-Alf realm. [4]

Known bordering realms: Earth, Mer, Salmhalla, Mer, and Tique (described as a hostile realm [5]).

(Cont. next page; Known Species)

[1]Read Kainan's Guide to Dur-Alf; Eden of the Realms

[2]Read Emily Randalp's Memoirs Among the Sprites

[3]Read Yin's Volume VI of Realm Studies Pages 1289 to 1402

[4]Read Consociation Guidelines for Interrealm Treaties. Page 157.

[5]Read Yin's Volume VIII of Realm Studies Page 44 to 399

Haven

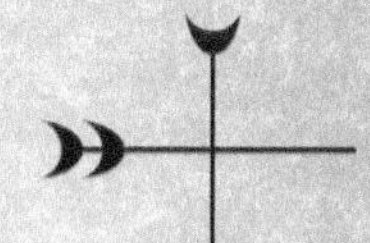

  Visible indication is a white mist of a thick consistency reminding some observers of cotton candy.

  Haven is a plane realm of breathable air, moisture in the form of clouds or mist, and no gravity. The ambient light is bright. No lifeforms or other identifying components have been found in the realm. [1][2][3]

  Dwarves and Merfolk have often used Earth merely to experience the realm. [3][4] Other than the magic available by touching the realm, little of use exists there.

  Hypothesises exist as to alternates states. [3][5][6]

  Known bordering realms: Earth, Salmhalla, and Tarus.

  (Cont. next page; Consociation Prohibitions)

---

[1] Read Yin's Volume III of Realm Studies. Pages 239 to 449 and appendix A

[2] Read Macrin's A Bridge to Haven; the Trail of Tears and Tribulations

[3] Read Innatala's Forgotten Path

[4] Read Soen's Research on Haven

[5] Read Ilionor's Mystics Realm

[6] Read Iai's Casual Observances and Lost Myths

Mer / Ishi-Iyai-Eyai-I

Visible indication is a blue-green liquid of a denser consistency than water.

Mer is a planet realm, a water-encased world with islands and some non-aquatic life. [1] Mer is the third planet from a hot star with higher than Earth surface temperatures and a single satellite. [2] Like Earth's humans, merfolk are the single indigenous intelligent life. Non-indigenous sentient life include the porpoises and whales, two of the numerous transplanted species between the two realms. [2]

No reported excursions into the realm have survived, and the merfolk refuse access to the realm, part of their reasoning for joining the Consociation.

Known bordering realms: Dur-Alf, Earth, and Tarus.

Interrealm travel from Earth by humans is prohibited by the Consociation Regulations. [4]

(Cont. next page; historical connection to Earth and Dur-Alf)

[1] Read Sienna's Treatise on Mer Isolation

[2] Read Tino Vangian Biography of Venis: Traitor of Mer

[6] Read Consociation Guidelines for Interrealm Treaties. Page 114.

Salmhalla

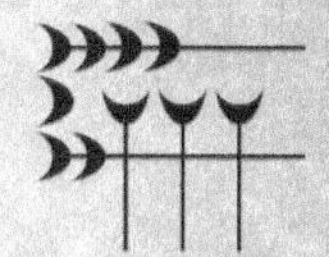

Indications include a liquid gold which is burning hot to the touch. [1]

Salmhalla is a plane of ambient sunlight and hot air temperatures. [1] [2] The plane contains a wide range of Earth-like terrains but predominantly includes mountains and grassy hills. [1] [2] [3] Several large water bodies have been detailed, but none rise to the level of oceans. [2] [3] [4] [5]

Consociation guidelines prohibit interaction with the realm and dragons enforce this edict. [6]

Known infringements have resulted in death, disappearance, mental illness, and loss of memory.

(Cont. next page; Known, theorized, and postulated magics connected to the Salmhalla realm)

[1] Read Yin's Volume IV of Realm Studies. Pages 1121 to 1349 and appendix C

[2] Read Inhai Du Anya's Scriptures of the High Dragons. Pages 89 to 97.

[3] Read Serjin's Testimonials

[4] Read Ilionor's Biography of Reshin. Pages 245 to 271.

[5] Read Wooley's Anecdotal Studies of Salmhalla

[6] Read Consociation Guidelines for Interrealm Treaties. Page 57.

Tarus

Visible indications are a dark-gray color and a misty consistency with glittering elements akin pin head .

Tarus is a plane realm with no ambient lighting and an oxygen-rich atmosphere. [1][2] Theories vary that the indigenous lifeforms have abilities to perceive lower frequency magnetic waves, have other senses, or solely rely on tactile and auditory senses. [2][3] [4] Most grimoires record little of verifiable evidence, but specimens from the realm have been studied extensively by multiple races.[5][6] A rocky, waterless terrain is a commonly accepted description. [2][4]

Known bordering realms: Earth, Haven, and Ya Keya.

(Cont. next page; Consociation Prohibitions)

[1]Read Yin's Volume II of Realm Studies. Pages 71 to 549 and appendix B

[2]Read Rasputin's Walks Among the Undead, the annotated version.

[3]Read Serjin's Agreements in Darkness

[4]Read Ilionor's Dedication

[5]Read Finyai's Tarus Biology

[6]Read Ted Dansworth's Research of Tarus Corporeal

Ya Keya

Indications include a light gray mist which is moist to the touch.

Considered the hunter's dream world , it is a plane of blue gray twilight according to numerous excursions including a Merfolk expedition led by Antre.[1] The plane contains a wide range of Earth-like terrains but predominantly includes forests, plains, and savannahs. No large water bodies have ever been detailed, but marshes and bogs were noted. [2]

Continued interaction with the plane consistently results in a transmutation on a cellular level and the werewolf's bodily fluids become contagious.[3] Longevity and increased metabolic functions have been studied extensively. [4] [5]

Witches and Merfolk have lost all abilities to interact with the realms once transmutation has occurred.

(Cont. next page; Known Inhabitants of Ya Keya)

[1] Read Antre's paper on *To Ya Keya: Sacrifice and Betrayal*

[2] Read Yin's *Volume III of Realm Studies*

[3] Read Jayne Dunham's *Voyage Home*

[4] Read Kizurra's *History of Akkadian Werewolves - the Dawn*

[5] Read Demot's *Monograph* for an in-depth biological reference

ALSO BY KEVIN A DAVIS

Please head to my website and join my mailing list if you'd like to be kept up to date on this series or my other books.

DRC Files - An episodic paranormal procedural series

Book One: Atlanta's Guide to Cryptids

Book Two: Tallahassee's Manual on Arcane Artifacts

Khimmer Chronicles - contemporary fantasy with magic and cryptids in modern day Tallahassee, Florida

"A plucky protagonist who's still finding her way propels this fantasy adventure." Kirkus

https://www.kirkusreviews.com/book-reviews/kevin-a-davis/wights-wrath/

Wight's Wrath - Book One

Death's Contract - Book Two

Fate's Betrayal - Book Three

High Fae's Quest - Book Four

Friday's Fifth - Book Five

Nyx's Blade - The Origin Story

Find out more

Website KevinArthurDavis.com

Facebook @KevinArthurDavis

KevinADavis on Instagram

KevinADavisUF on Twitter

Acknowledgments

April still enjoys the DRC files despite all my constant babbling about it and the multiple times she was asked to read it. Her proofing has caught a number of errors which would have gone to print.

Robyn Huss, my editor, weaves her own magic on my stories. If you enjoy this, it's largely due to her. If you're a writer, I encourage you to look at some of the opportunities she offers - http://www.hussediting.com/

The Fireside Group; Tim, Siena, Rosemary, Mark, Vail, and Katharine keep me challenged to do better. Arrash and Michele from Jody Lynn Nye's DragonCon workshop keep me on task with the most intricate details and loving support. Dianne and Brett from Apex have been there for me.

I still miss David Farland's gentle mentorship. Please pick up one of his books and enjoy the magic he endowed upon the world. Writers, study his lessons at Apex Writers.

Jody Lynn Nye's Dragoncon workshop will always be my go to suggestion for an in-person critique for any aspiring writers. Her insight is invaluable.

The wonderful cover art is by MIBLart! Consider them for your next design.

Thank you.

About the Author

Kevin A Davis is an author from north Florida who travels the southeast United States to vend, speak, and sometimes just as a fan of nerdy conventions.

The AngelSong series and the Khimmer Chronicles are completed series which you can find in paper, audio, and digital. The DRC Files is an episodic series with no completion arc planned. Hopefully, you've enjoyed this book.

Reviews are helpful on Goodreads and Amazon, but especially to your like-minded friends.

Works in progress include a YA shifter romance and an Epic Fantasy series while episodes 3&4 of the DRC Files are completed and await their editor.

Please follow and find out more
  Website KevinArthurDavis.com
  Facebook @KevinArthurDavis
  KevinADavis on Instagram
  KevinADavisUF on Twitter
  @inkdpub on TikTok

9 7 9 8 9 8 9 2 8 1 0 4 6